THE
MIGHTY
SKINK

THE MIGHTY SKINK

PAUL SHIPTON

HarperCollins*Publishers*

Library of Congress Cataloging-in-Publication Data
Shipton, Paul.
The mighty skink / by Paul Shipton.
p. cm.
Summary: A young rhesus monkey living in a zoo enclosure with the rest
of his tribe finds all his ideas about tribal order,
the superiority of humans, and the wonders of the outside world challenged
by the arrival of a new, seemingly unprepossessing, monkey with radical ideas.
ISBN 0-688-17420-5
[1. Monkeys—Fiction. 2. Zoos—Fiction. 3. Bullies—Fiction. 4. Interpersonal relations—
Fiction. 5. Conduct of life—Fiction.] I. Title. PZ7.S55765 Mi 2000 [Fic]—dc21 99-46186

1 2 3 4 5 6 7 8 9 10
❖
First Edition

For my mum and dad

–P.S.

ONE

I REMEMBER the day Skink arrived like it only just happened. I remember it so well because it was the day that things changed forever.

I spent the morning just swinging around the outer branches of the Big Tree. It was my most favorite spot in the whole world. Every once in awhile, I let out this great big whoop, like this: *WHOOOOOOOOOO-UP! WHOOOOOOOO-UP!*

It's not easy to get a whoop just right. You've got to start right deep down in your belly, then kind of build up in your chest, so it gets louder and louder, until it rises at the end for that final -*UP!*

You know, a whoop like that can express a lot of different feelings: It all comes down to how you make it. The only thing is, I couldn't really tell you what my calls were saying that day—a whole bunch of thoughts, all mixed up. "Wondering" whoops, I guess you could call them. See, I wanted to get some good thinking done, and you couldn't get much brain work done down on the ground with the rest of the Tribe all chattering around you and making a racket. That's why the Big Tree was really good—you could scoot up it and almost feel like you were on your own. But the best thing was, it had this great view of what was outside the Enclosure. What I'd do, I'd climb up to my branch and spend hours just looking out across the Fence.

Chim, who was my best friend—even though I'd never tell him that in a million years—he always said that I spent too much time thinking. He said that I'd wear my brain out with thinking too much, and I'd end up this crazy old monkey that couldn't even unzip a banana for myself. Ha!

Me, I didn't care. I just liked hanging there and looking out beyond the Fence. I got a good view of the lions behind their own fence, and I could see the lanky outlines of the giraffes in the fields in the distance. Sure, I liked to look at the other animals and wonder about them and stuff, but that's not what I was really interested in, which was what lay *beyond* all the other enclosures. You know, *out there*. I thought about it so often, it made my head itch on the inside. What's it like out there . . . out in the land of humans? I knew I would have to get old Graybak to tell me again the stories he'd heard of what there was beyond all the enclosures.

This sudden clanking noise interrupted me right in midthink. I knew what it was—no mistaking that sound. The movable section of the Fence was creaking and rolling to one side. The gap it left could only mean one thing: The Guards were letting someone in. Humans were arriving! Brilliant! I swung down on the branch, so I was just hanging by one arm, and I looked over to where the humans were coming into the Enclosure.

As usual, they were in one of those big *car* things. Of course, the rest of the Tribe had noticed, and they were all watching and whooping and hollering like crazy. I dropped to the ground—THUNK!—and started charging toward the car, which had stopped moving now. A bunch of other young monkeys was running toward it as well—about five of us, I guess, all from different parts of the Enclosure, and one of them was Chim. The little monkey was giggling like he was nutty, which he was. He grinned when he spotted me, and he scrunched up his little monkey face and scampered faster.

"Hey, Flea Face!" he yelled. He usually called me "Flea Face" or something like that, instead of my proper name, which is Kaz. "Last one there's a peanut brain!" His giggle went up a couple of notches. I put on a burst of speed. Chim was closer, but I was faster and I reached the car first. I hopped up onto the big flat part at the front and took a good long look at the humans inside.

There were four of them in there, all wearing those things they like to cover themselves with—you know, *clothes*. (Who knows why? I mean, what are they trying to hide?) The fully grown humans were sitting up front. The Woman was gripping a big wheel thing in both hands, and the Man was just sitting there with his face looking all weird and hairless, the way humans do. The ones in the backseat were smaller—young ones—and they were staring back at me and giggling. Chim was giggling, too. He had hopped onto the car as well now and was jigging around beside me. Three more monkeys were on top, all screeching their heads off.

When I'd had myself a good look at the humans, I joined in with the other monkeys. Which is to say, I started hopping and jigging and gyrating around on the car, too. That's what the young monkeys always did when a car came through the Enclosure. We're *supposed* to do it. The idea, according to the Tales of Why Things Came to Be, is that dancing around like that is a way of giving thanks to the humans, because they feed us and they gave us the Fence and all that stuff. This is the Tale, which I know word for word because I only heard it about eight million times when I was little:

Way back in the long ago, when the World Forest was young, all the animals lived together. The monkey lived side by side with all the other beasts. But all was not well in the Forest—many of the animals wanted to hunt and devour the monkey, who was generally considered quite tasty. The poor old monkey lived in a world of hungry jaws.

But Human, who was first and best and wisest of all the animals, took pity on the monkey. It said that the monkey reminded him of itself, in a funny kind of way. And so it built the Fence, and filled it with the power of Electricity. Then it placed the monkey inside the Fence, and decreed that we were never to leave this Enclosure. It

would bring us food here and keep us safe. And
inside, we would be free from the jaws and claws
of the other beasts—only Human would visit us
in here. (Well, the birds could, too, but they don't
count because they're so dumb.)

And that is why, whenever humans come to
visit in their cars, we dance to honor them, and
give thanks for the Fence.

That's how the Tale goes, anyway. I don't know
about all that; I just know jumping on cars is fun.

So there I was on the front of the car. I was just
going into this tricky move, which was spinning
around and grabbing my tail with my foot, when
another monkey joined me. It was Blok! He was the
biggest of us Second Order monkeys, which is to say,
he was the biggest of us monkeys not yet old enough
to join the Council of Adults. Blok grunted and gave
me this great big whack right on the head with one
of his meaty fists. It was about three thousand times
harder than it needed to be, but he wanted to make
it clear who was Top Monkey around here—*him.*

"Learn your place, Kaz," he said, and he deliv-
ered it with a kind of snarl—all mean and tough-
sounding. Then he took up the best position on the

car, right in front of the big see-through bit that the humans look out of, which is called a *window*. That was where I'd been standing.

I tried to look like I didn't care, but my head was smarting big time, and that's no lie. I hopped up onto the top and across to the back of the car. I let out a sort of party whoop, but my heart wasn't really in it anymore. That's when I noticed this sign stuck on the back of the car: a white sign with black and red squiggles, which is what the humans call *writing* (whatever *that* is). The sign looked like this:

I ❤ BRODER ZOO

What did it mean? I didn't have a clue, but there was something mysterious and wonderful about it. I traced the squiggles with my finger.

Just then, the car made a different rumbling noise. That meant it was going to start moving again, and, sure enough, it did. Chim, who's a scaredy-monkey even though he likes to pretend he isn't, screamed and leapt off. So did the three monkeys on top of the car. But I was so interested in the sign that I stayed on longer than I should. Meanwhile, the car picked up speed. When I looked down, the ground was whizzing by, and that's when I jumped.

It was only when I hit the ground that I realized that I'd stayed on the car longer than Blok. Ooops. That was bad.

The thing you've got to know about life in the Tribe is that everyone knows their rank. So, the adult monkeys of the First Order are the highest rank, which means they get first choice of food and where to sleep and all that. Then it's us—the Second Order—the monkeys not old enough to have our say on the Council. And then the Third Order, which is everyone else—you know, the old monkeys and the very young ones, and so on. The Rules of how to behave are totally strict, and just about the worst thing you can do is insult a monkey who outranks you.

But that's what I'd just done.

You see, even within your own order, you have to know your place and show respect. Well, Blok was Top Monkey in our order, and that meant he outranked me. And *that* meant that if, say, we both wanted the same piece of food, Blok would get it. It also meant that when we were on a human's car, Blok got to stay on it longer than I did. Those were the Rules, and breaking them was like issuing a challenge to Blok.

So that's why the big monkey was giving me one of his angry stares, and I felt this feeling of fear giving my gut a squeeze. I reckoned it would be smart to hide right about now—before Blok got to me, that is. I made a dash to the shrubbery, and Chim followed.

Once we'd reached some cover, I glanced back. I was pretty scared, I guess, but Blok hadn't bothered to follow. He knew he could wait. Chim and I were right near the Fence now. Of course, we didn't actually touch it—we weren't that stupid. We both knew that a powerful force lived inside the Fence. Electricity. We just sat and watched as the car moved off, back toward the Guards' building. One Guard always stands there by the gate to make sure none of us has stayed on a car. They needn't bother—everyone knows that's against the Rules. Then the car went out of the Enclosure, and away to whatever lay beyond. I watched it go until it was nothing more than a dinky little red dot moving across the giraffe fields.

"What's out there, do you think?" I asked Chim at last.

"Out where?" Chim grinned, showing all his teeth, and did a back flip, which I took as a sign that he hadn't given the question his full consideration.

"You know, out beyond the Fence? Past all of the enclosures?"

Chim thought about it for a while. He was trying hard this time, I knew—these two little lines of concentration appeared on his forehead. At last, he spoke. "Stuff," he said.

"Stuff, like what?"

Chim gave me one of his special Chimmy shrugs. "You think too much, Kaz—who cares what's out there? You think too much, and you think about the wrong stuff . . ." Then he gave this sly grin. I knew what that little smirk meant—Chim had something to tell me.

"What do you mean, bumhead?" I asked politely.

Chim swished his tail back and forth like a big shot, and he half-chanted, "I know something you don't know . . ." This was how Chim had always told me things, ever since we were both babies clinging to our mothers' backs. Sometimes it made me laugh, and sometimes it drove me nuts . . . like today.

"*What* do you know?" I demanded. I plucked a flea from the top of my friend's head and popped it into my mouth. It was a good one—nice and crunchy, the way I like 'em.

Chim kept his smirk going. I let him squeeze out

the last few drops of satisfaction. I knew he couldn't hold in the secret much longer.

"There's a new monkey arriving," he said at last, and he puffed out his hairy little chest. "Due to get here this afternoon."

Chim's grin stretched even wider. This was big news all right. I didn't know the last time a monkey had arrived from outside the Fence. I wasn't sure it had *ever* happened.

"How did you find out?" I asked him.

Chim shrugged. "I was just . . . you know . . . hanging around over by the rocks. . . ." I knew it! The rocks were the meeting place for the Council of Adults, which led our Tribe. It was absolutely, completely, totally out of bounds to us younger monkeys, but that didn't stop Chim.

"Just hanging around having a good snoop, eh?"

Another shrug. "Anyway, I heard Kalibak telling the Council."

Kalibak was the biggest, toughest monkey of all, and so, no great surprise, he was the Leader of the Tribe. The Council of Adults was supposed to vote on every important decision, but everyone knew Kalibak's word was what mattered. We all knew not to cross him. Chim had been taking a big chance.

"I don't get it. What happens when a new monkey arrives?" he asked me.

I didn't know the answer, but I had an idea who would.

"Graybak," I said.

TWO

I DIDN'T think lunchtime would ever arrive.

But then the gate rolled back and the Guards drove into the Enclosure in their big car, which is called a *truck*. One of them stood in the back by the food container and scattered our lunch all over the place. As usual, the whole Tribe let out this great big cheer and dropped out of the trees like falling fruit and began to stuff their faces. We were no exception. Chim shoved so many grapes into his mouth that his neck pouches were bulging, and then he shoved a few more in. I scanned the Enclosure for Graybak.

He was over on the east side, moving slowly and peering down at the ground like he couldn't tell for sure what was food and what was ground. His eyes weren't so good anymore.

I ran to him. "Graybak," I said, "I brought you

something." I held out the ear of corn, good and close so he could tell what it was.

The old monkey raised his head, which was all gray and grizzled on account of how old he is. He smiled. Corn was his favorite food.

"You're a good boy, Kaz."

It was funny to think that Graybak had once been young and strong and healthy and all that stuff. Now he was so old and weak he couldn't even climb a tree anymore. That's why he was in the Third Order, which meant that, along with the all the other weak or sick monkeys, he had to make do with the food no one else wanted—the crummy stuff, like sprouts. An ear of corn was a real treat.

I liked to bring him something nice like this most days, because when I was little, Graybak had looked after me when my parents had passed away—which is a nice way of saying died—from the Flu.

Graybak munched on the corn, and I could tell from all the slurping noises that he liked it. I let him eat in peace, which is to say, I didn't bug him with twenty thousand questions or so while he ate, even though I wanted to.

When he was done, he looked up at me with those bluish, filmy eyes of his. "So . . . what's new, sonny?"

"You know—this and that." I shrugged, though I knew it wasn't much of an answer, so I added, "I've been thinking."

Graybak shook his head and smiled. "There you go again, Kaz. Still wasting your time on all the Big Questions that you'll never find an answer to. . . ."

That's what Graybak always called them: my "Big Questions"—things like *Have the Rules always been the same? Who made them and why?* And, of course, the biggest of the Big Questions: *What's it like out there, beyond the Fence?*

Graybak did his best to be stern and disapproving when I asked him about stuff like that, but I knew that he didn't really mind. I think he liked it, in fact, and there was one story in particular that he enjoyed telling me, even though he'd never admit it.

"Go on, let me hear it one more time," I said. "Tell me the story of the monkey who got out . . ."

Graybak let out a long sigh, like this *fffssshhhh,* as if he didn't really want to tell me again, even though we both knew this was a big act. When he thought he'd put up enough of a fuss, he got down to telling me the story.

"Well, this happened many years ago, you understand. Life wasn't the same around here. I was just a kid, no bigger than you. We had a decent-enough Leader back then, not some bully boy who thinks he can boss the whole Tribe around." He winked at me, and I knew he was talking about Kalibak, who Graybak didn't much care for. "The Fence wasn't so powerful back then, and there were antelope in the next enclosure, not lions. Well, anyway, there was this headstrong young monkey in our order who dreamed of seeing what was out there, over the Fence and beyond the enclosures. Of course, dreaming is one thing and doing is another. But one day it came to him—a plan for how to do it."

"What was his plan?" I asked in this awed whisper.

"Couldn't tell you," answered the old monkey. "Only that it worked—and he made it to the other side of the Fence. Well, he had himself a look at the other animals in their enclosures—the hippos and the zebras and the giraffes. And then he went farther . . . out into the world of humans."

I leaned forward. This was the best bit.

"He didn't get very far before he was caught," continued the old monkey, "but he came back with amazing stories of what he'd seen—humans everywhere, big old buildings full of them. Enormous roads, too, far bigger than the piddly little one that runs through here, that they zoom along on in their cars. . . ."

"What about other animals?"

"Didn't see many. He said there were dogs walking with the humans, but the dogs had something tied round their necks so the humans could control them." I'd heard of dogs, of course, but imagine seeing them!

"Wow," I whispered. It was hard even to picture it—*out there.*

"Don't you ever wish you could see it yourself?" I asked. "Know what there is beyond the Fence?"

Graybak reached a finger into his mouth to get a bit of corn that was stuck between his teeth. "Nah . . ." he said. "There's more important things for me to be thinking about—like what goes on here. And the same goes for you, too, sonny boy . . ."

I couldn't wait any longer, and that's when I blurted, "A new monkey's going to arrive . . . today!" Graybak nodded like he knew all about it, though I didn't see how he could.

"Has that ever happened before?" I asked. "Has a new monkey ever come here?"

The old monkey just shook his head in this thoughtful way he had of shaking his head.

"Not for as long as I can remember," he said, and

I knew that was a *long* time. Graybak was the oldest monkey in the whole Tribe. Once—ages ago—he had actually been Leader. But that was before he had become all old and weak—before the young and strong Kalibak had kicked him off the top spot and taken over.

A lion from the next enclosure let out this great big roar, which made me jump. I looked around. In the distance, the big cats were lying around as usual. One of them let out another lazy half roar, half yawn. I was glad that the Fence around our Enclosure and the one that encircled theirs lay between us. Graybak didn't even flinch. I guess he had heard a lot of roars in his time.

"But when the new monkey gets here," I began, "what if—"

I didn't get to finish my question. Right then, the Guards' truck rumbled into the Enclosure again. There was something on the back of it, but it wasn't food this time. It was a box, which a Guard held steady as the truck rattled and bounced and clattered over the bumpy ground.

They stopped near the sleeping huts, which are for monkeys who don't like snoozing up in the trees. One of the humans opened up the front of the box.

I followed every move and realized I was holding my breath. At first, nothing came out of the box, but then a weedy-looking arm appeared. The rest of the monkey's body followed.

"What's going on, lad?" said Graybak. What with his rotten eyesight, he couldn't make things out so far away.

"It's the new monkey; he's here!" I said. "And he looks like a pretty skinny little guy." It was true—the new arrival wasn't too impressive to look at—not from this distance, at any rate. Bigger than Chim perhaps, but not as big as me (and I'm not all that big for a Second Order monkey).

The truck rumbled off and left the new arrival looking all small and alone. But he didn't seem too concerned. Just the opposite, in fact. He looked around slowly. Then he arched his back and reached his arms out in this big, just-woken-up stretch, with a yawn thrown in.

I couldn't wait to talk to the newcomer, but I knew I would *have* to wait. Nobody would be able to approach him until Kalibak and the Council had spoken to the new monkey. Those were the Rules, and I wasn't in the mood to break any more that day. Bad enough that I'd gone and insulted Blok. The last thing I needed was to bring Kalibak's anger crashing down on me, too.

I kept on watching. Sure enough, a fully grown, First Order monkey strolled right on up to the newcomer. I told Graybak what was happening.

"Must be saying that the Council wants to see him," said the old monkey. I looked over at the rocks. Kalibak and his Council were waiting there silently. All sitting on the rocks like that, they looked . . . well, they looked like a bunch of monkeys sitting on some rocks, I suppose. But there was something creepy about it, too, if you know what I mean.

Back near the huts, Kalibak's messenger spoke. I don't know what he said, but the newcomer broke into this huge grin, and then he threw his head back and laughed. The messenger didn't join in. Then the newcomer nodded and followed him over to the rocks where the Council was waiting.

"Just think," I said. "He's come from the *other side* of the Fence. He's been *out there*. He knows what it's like!"

"See what I mean, Kaz," said the old monkey. "Still chasing those Big Questions. . . . Get them out of your head, boy!"

That was all very well—but how could I?

It seemed like Kalibak and the Council spent forever talking to the new monkey. I couldn't think about much else, and the afternoon just crept by second by second. To make matters worse, a gang of old gray clouds had shoved aside the sun, and a nasty wind had gotten up. It made the wires of the Fence sway and hum, like this *vvvvmmmm,* which is a nice sound, until you remember what's making it.

I sat at the edge of the road that winds through the Enclosure. I was keeping an eye out for Blok, but I was most interested in the rocks, where the Council was still questioning the new monkey. Chim squatted near me. Every so often, he'd pick up a clump of grass and throw it at the side of my head. He wasn't such a great shot, but I wasn't very good at dodging when my mind was on other things.

"What are you thinking, banana-skin-head?" Chim asked at last.

"About the new monkey."

Chim treated me to one of his Chimmy smirks. That made me mad.

"Oh yeah? And what should I be thinking about, smart-monkey?" I scooped up a handful of dirt and let fly. I was a better shot than Chim, always had been, and I caught him a good one.

"Oy!" yelled Chim, laughing. "Lucky for you it only hit my head!"

It struck me that what old Chim really needed right then was a good tickling, and I was just the monkey to dish it out. I started toward him, but for some reason, he'd lost his grin. He wasn't even looking at me; he was looking *behind* me—

That's when I felt the heavy tap on my shoulder. I turned, and there I was staring up into a pair of mean, close-set eyes—Blok. The big monkey bared his teeth.

"We have unfinished business, Kaz," he said.

I didn't have to guess—he meant what had happened on the car that morning, when I'd broken the Rules and insulted Blok, the Top Monkey in our order. Now it was time to pay the price. . . .

My first thought was to leg it, but I knew that wouldn't help—Blok was faster than you'd expect. I wasn't certain I *could* outrun him. Besides, he'd be sure to catch up with me sometime. Fear began to clutch and squeeze inside my belly again. I willed my legs to stop trembling, but they ignored me and went right on trembling anyway.

"Leave him alone, Blok," said Chim. It was nice of him to chip in, but I noticed that he had backed off to a safe distance.

"You keep out of this, squirt," said Blok. He didn't shift his gaze from me. "This is between me and Kaz. . . ."

A group of young monkeys started to gather round us—everyone likes to see a good scrap.

I held my hands open wide, like I was offering him something, although the only thing I had to offer was an explanation. "Listen. About this morning . . . it was a mistake. You see, I—"

He waved my words aside like they were a cloud of pesky mosquitoes. "I don't care! The Rules are the Rules, and you're going to have to learn what your place is in this order. . . ." He flattened back his ears, which meant he was ready to attack. I didn't stand a chance. I got ready for the worst.

But it never came, because an unfamiliar voice interrupted us: "Hey, boys. What's going on here?"

We all whirled around. It was the new monkey—the Council must have finished with him. He strolled up to us, nibbling on a banana. I'd been right the first time: He *was* one scrawny, skinny little monkey, and what's more, his fur wasn't in the best shape. It was hard to put an age on him. But there was something about his eyes, the way they sparkled and shone with this fierce light—that sounds weird, I know, but it's the only way I can describe it, "fierce"—as if he was laughing at some joke that only he knew.

"Hey, you're the new monkey!" piped up Chim.

"No flies on you, big guy," said the new monkey. "You must be the brains of this outfit." Chim cracked a big grin. The newcomer nodded at us all. "The name's Skink."

"What kind of stupid name is that?" demanded Blok. He was still in a fighting mood and he had reached the stage where he didn't care *who* he fought. This skinny newcomer with the silly name would do just as well.

The new monkey was unfazed. "Only one I've got," he answered, and he was still all smiles. "What do they call you?"

"Blok."

"Hoo-eee," declared Skink, still in that relaxed, friendly tone. "And look who's saying *I've* got a silly name!"

Blok blinked for a few moments before he twigged that this scrawny little stranger was insulting him. He forgot about me and took a step toward the newcomer. I jumped in before Blok tried to begin his second fight of the day.

"My name's Kaz," I said, "and this is—"

"Chim!" piped up Chim.

The other monkeys there said hi, too, and I thought for a moment that we were going to get away without any fighting. Big mistake, because the next thing the monkey named Skink said was, "So . . . who's Top Monkey around these parts?" He still sounded all buddy-buddy, like he didn't know he was asking for trouble.

Blok drew himself up to his full height, which was pretty tall. The newcomer looked puny next to him—Skink's head only came up to Blok's barrel chest.

"*I'm* Top Monkey," growled Blok. He flexed his muscles and flicked his tail.

Skink gave us onlookers a big friendly wink.

"Not anymore," he said.

THREE

"**THIS GUY** must be crazy," whispered Chim out of the corner of his mouth. "He must *want* to die."

Me, I wasn't so sure. Okay, Blok was much bigger, and it wasn't hard to see that he was much stronger. And yet . . . there was something about that look in Skink's eyes that made me think he was a match for Blok. *More* than a match.

A dark expression flashed across Skink's face. For a moment, I thought he was going to launch himself at the bigger monkey. But then the moment passed, and that friendly grin was back.

"Tell you what," Skink said. "I've had a long journey today, I'm not much in the mood for a fight. . . ."

"Big shock," scoffed Blok, and all his pals who'd shown up guffawed along with him. "What, are you scared or something, skinny?"

"Nope, but I'm more in the mood for another kind of challenge." Skink grinned. "Something to prove my worth, if you get my meaning. . . ."

What did he mean? Even Blok was curious. "What kind of challenge?" he asked.

Skink leaned back. "Well, what do you do for fun around here?"

Blok didn't answer. To him, what he was doing right then was fun—getting ready to beat up one monkey or another. I thought I'd better say something, so I told Skink what happened when human visitors came through in their cars.

"But they never leave the cars?" Skink asked. Fires of mischief did this little dance in his eyes.

"Of course they never leave the cars!" snapped Blok. He was losing patience, and when Blok lost patience, a punch-up was never far away. "They're humans! They come in through the Fence, they stop for a few minutes, and then they go again! That's it!"

Blok's voice was getting to sound all angry, but Skink just nodded pleasantly, like they were old friends having a chat over a banana or two.

"Okay, then," he said at last, "how about this for a challenge? Before the afternoon is over, I'll get one human to leave its car."

"Impossible!" sputtered Blok. "It wouldn't happen, it can't, it's—"

"So does that mean you accept?" said Skink.

Blok glared, said nothing.

"What, are you scared or something, chunky?" Skink beamed.

I heard Chim let out a little gasping *eep* that was halfway between fear and astonishment. Nobody called Blok a coward and got away with it.

"I accept," Blok said at last. Then he pushed his face closer to Skink's, so that their noses almost touched. "And by the end of the afternoon, when you've failed . . . you're *mine.*"

Then he spun around and stalked off to the trees. His three buddies went with him. We watched them swagger away.

"Nice guy," declared Skink, giving us a wink.

Chim let out a snicker, but I figured the newcomer needed to be clued in before he made any more mistakes.

"Don't be fooled," I said. "Blok's big and dim, but he can be dangerous. He's the nephew of Kalibak, our Leader, *and* he's Top Monkey in the Second Order, which means that he'll become Leader of the Tribe one day, when we're old enough to move up a rank.

What I'm saying is, you don't want him for an enemy."

Skink gave his lower lip a tug. "Thanks," he said, "but don't worry about me. I can look after myself. And as for 'one day' . . ."

He let the comment hang in midair and jumped up to his feet. "So . . . are you boys going to help me make good on this challenge?"

Chim was hopping anxiously from foot to foot, like he needed to take a wee. "Well, er . . ." That's Chim—he talks a good game, but he's a wimp when it comes down to it.

Me, I figured I owed the newcomer. After all, he'd stopped Blok from starting a fight with me—a fight I was sure to lose, by the way.

"What can we do?" I asked.

Skink grinned. "Well, you can take this banana. . . ."

Once everything was ready, we plopped ourselves down in the middle of the Enclosure, alongside the road, and waited. When the weather was bad like today, not so many humans came through the Fence to look at us. Who knew why?

Of course, I didn't mind waiting. I had this

gigantic list of questions to start on.

"So where were you before here?" I asked.

"Oh, lots of places."

And all of them out there on the other side of the Fence! added this little voice inside my brain.

"Like where?"

"You know, here and there, this place and that. But, I tell you, I've never been anywhere quite like this. . . ."

"What do you mean?" I asked.

"You know, all these animals. When they brought me in, I got a good look at everything. There's a lot more here than you can see from this Enclosure. I saw a couple of elephants lifting logs, and we drove past this huge field full of zebras and gazelles. I saw a pool with this big ol' hippo wallowing around."

I listened, all eager. Of course, we knew there were other enclosures; we could see one or two of them. And we knew that some of the land around the enclosures was for humans only—you could watch them driving around from spot to spot, looking at the animals.

"What else?" I asked.

"Well, let's see—the lions, you know about. I saw some emus, a couple of vultures, some giraffes. I guess there's even a building with snakes and a croc-odile. . . ."

"Really? A crocodile?" This was news to me. According to the Tales, the crocodile was the most dangerous of all the animals, but also the most knowledgeable . . . after humans, of course. This was how the story went:

Way, way back in the long ago, when all the animals lived together, the creatures of the world were very different from how they are now. But slowly they changed—those who preferred the cold grew thicker fur; those who didn't want to be seen developed camouflage; those who were hunters developed sharper teeth and speed for the chase; and those who were the hunted developed speed for the escape. Of course, humans changed most of all. But the crocodile never changed one bit—it didn't need to. It was happy in the rivers, it got all the food it needed, and the armor-plated monster was content to stay the same as ever. It just watched the change all around it . . . and remembered everything. And that's why the crocodile is known as the greatest historian of all the animals, as well as one of the most dangerous.

I told Skink this Tale, and he nodded all the way through like he was hearing it for the first time, which I guess he was.

After that, I got the feeling he didn't want to talk much anymore, which was frustrating, but I figured we'd have plenty of time later. So we sat in silence and listened to the wind and the chattering of the Tribe around us. After a while, Skink began to hum under his breath, some song I'd never heard before.

"What's that?" I asked.

I guess he didn't even know he'd been doing it. But then he cleared his throat and sang some words to go with the tune he'd been humming. His voice was good and clear, and the song went like this:

"Oh, life is a riddle
That you'll never work out.
But the monkey meets it
With a dance and a shout.
So when you climb that final tree
Take Sim a banana just for me!"

It was a neat tune, but there was something sad deep down at the heart of it. I couldn't put my finger on what.

"Who's Sim?" I asked.

But Skink was shaking his head. "No time for questions." He pointed toward the Guards' building by the Fence. A car was entering the Enclosure. "It's party time!"

After it passed through the open gate, the car had to bump and shake across this *grille* thing, which was like a bunch of metal sticks all lying in a row next to the Guards' hut. That part of the Enclosure, near the gap in the Fence, was called "No Monkey's Land," because the Guards wouldn't let us anywhere near it.

"You two ready?" Skink asked us, his head bobbing up and down. I nodded. The car was getting closer. I could see three fleshy human faces pressing up against the windows and looking out at the monkeys that flopped and lounged about on the top of one sleeping hut.

"Let's go!" said Skink.

We scurried forward, keeping low and out of sight. When we got there, Chim leapt up onto the front of the car and began spinning around chattering his teeth, same as usual. That was his job—to keep those humans happy and distracted. Skink and I crept to the side of the car. He pointed to one of the four round things that the car had at each corner.

"See the black parts on the outside of the wheels?" he said. "They're called *tires.*" I nodded like I understood. "This is what you do," continued Skink. He ran forward and plucked off this little round thing from the inside of the wheel. Then he pressed the knobbly bit with one long, thin finger. The tire began to give out a hissing noise.

"They're filled with air," he explained. "That's how they work." Sure enough, the tire's shape was changing. Before it had been firm and round, but now it was beginning to look flat on the bottom as the air rushed out.

I dashed to the other wheel on this side and did the same thing. I wasn't as fast as Skink, but it worked well enough. More air began to hiss out.

"Now what?"

Skink let out a wild laugh. "Now for phase two."

We jumped up onto the front of the car, where Chim was busy waving his tail and bottom at the humans inside. They were laughing away at him, *ho, ho, ho.* Skink marched up the front of the car and took hold of one of the long stick things there.

"This is called a *windshield wiper,*" he said. He began to yank back on it with all his wiry strength. "You get the other one." I took hold of the other stick thing and pulled it back and forth. It sounded cool.

The adult male human inside the car wasn't laughing now. It looked all red, and it was pounding on the window with the flat of its hand. Chim waved back. I would have waved as well, but I was busy.

The human flopped back in its seat. It turned something in its hand and the car rumbled into life underneath us. It started to move, but Skink just laughed. "Stay put!" he called to Chim and me.

The car jerked forward, but there was a sound that was different from the usual one—like something wet and heavy slapping against the ground. *WHUMP! WHUMP!* It was the tires.

The human inside was looking madder and madder, redder and redder. It pressed down on something with its fist, and the car let out this loud noise: *BEEEP!* Then again, louder: *BEEEEEEEEEEP!*

That was the signal human visitors used when they wanted the Guards to come and help them. I looked across the Enclosure. The Guard looked up all startled, and the truck rumbled into life. But then the rumble coughed and sputtered, and then it died out altogether. The Guard hit the wheel in its hands—*it* didn't look very happy, either! Well, of course, it didn't know about the banana—the one

Skink had told me to stuff up the pipe at the back of the truck, which he said was called the *exhaust pipe.*

Meanwhile, Skink and I were doing a good job on the whatchamacallits—the windshield wipers. Skink's was almost clean off the car. He gave it one last mighty yank, and it came free. It made a neat sound, like this *SPROINNG!*

I glanced inside the car. The adult male human let out this furious shout, sort of "Aaargh!" Then it opened a gate on the side of the car, called a *door,* and leapt out. That's right, OUT OF THE CAR! Skink had won the challenge. The human looked very big and its hairless face looked very red. It was shouting something, but it just sounded like "BLAHBLAHBLAHBLAH!" which is how humans always sound.

Chim was the first away, and I was not far behind him. I thought we were done, but Skink hadn't finished yet. I looked back, and I couldn't believe what I saw. The tiny monkey was still on the car. He was gripping the wiper in his hand, waving it around like some kind of weapon, which he used to prod the human right in its big fat belly. He had actually struck a human, the greatest of all the animals!

It was too much for the human. It let out this

shriek and lunged for Skink. But of course, monkeys are way faster than humans. Skink back flipped off the car and out of danger. The human lurched around after him. Skink sat there as casual as could be, right until the last possible moment. Then he jumped away to a safe distance.

The chase went on like this for a good while. The whole Tribe was watching in amazement now as the pudgy human, who was soon puffing and panting, charged after the monkey. Blok was watching as well, and *he* didn't look too happy, either. Skink's laugh echoed around the trees.

The weird thing was, as well as the feeling of shock at what Skink had done, I felt something else. Watching the chase was . . . well, it was *funny,* to tell you the truth. I mean, we all knew that humans were the first and best and wisest of the animals—the Tales said so. But this human just looked so big and red and *stupid,* lolloping along after the monkey and shaking its fists. Was this the first and best and wisest of all the animals?

So anyway, by this time the Guard had figured out why the truck wouldn't go, and it had gotten rid of the banana. The truck started up again and this time did not die. The game would soon be over.

Right before the truck came to the rescue, Skink passed under the tree I was sitting in. He looked up for a second before he once again skipped out of the reach of the furious human. "Now *this* is what I call fun," he said, and he giggled fit to bust.

And do you know what? I giggled, too.

FOUR

NIGHT HAD fallen, and a fat yellow moon hung low in the sky. I was glad it was there to look down on us. Most of the monkeys had turned in for the night, sleeping either in the huts or up in the trees. Every so often some monkey let out a cry, like this *eeeeeeyip,* or sometimes *wheeeeeep.* Who knew what they saw in their dreams to make noises like that?

I knew one thing for sure—we were in trouble, me, Chim, and Skink. Most of all, Skink. The word was that Kalibak was furious. The Council was going to hold an emergency meeting first thing the next morning. We would have to go along to present our case and then, chances were, to hear our punishment.

Of course, I was thinking about what that punishment might be, but that wasn't the only thing on my mind as I sat in the branches. Lots of thoughts were sloshing around my brain, and I couldn't get a firm hold on any of them. The one that kept popping back into my mind was how *silly* the human had looked—not great, not wise. Just plain silly.

Finally, I gave up all hopes of trying to nod off to sleep (unlike Chim, who was snoring away in the next tree). I crept along my branch and shinnied down the trunk.

There weren't many monkeys still up and about. Those who were still awake sat in small huddles and spoke in quiet voices. I picked my way carefully across the Enclosure. The moon was sulking behind a bank of clouds now and didn't offer up much light, but that didn't matter—I knew every last blade of grass inside that Enclosure like the hairs on the back of my hand.

Something told me that Skink would be over near the Fence. Don't ask me how I knew, but I was right. He was leaning with his back up against an old tree stump, and a small group of monkeys was sitting around him. Skink's was the only voice I could hear. As I approached, I caught the last bit of some story he had been telling: ". . . and that's how we got away."

I settled in with the others—mostly young

monkeys, but with one or two adults mixed in. I was relieved to see that Blok wasn't around.

"Kaz." Skink grinned. "Glad you could join us!" He sounded as relaxed and cheerful as ever—you'd never imagine that we were going to be called before the Council the next morning.

One of the other monkeys piped up: "What I want to know is, why? Why did you do that today?" From the way she asked, I could tell she didn't approve but that she was intrigued as well. Like the rest of the monkeys there, I guessed.

Skink just smiled and scratched his head. "I don't see the big deal," he said. "What was so bad about it?"

"You dishonored a human!" said another monkey. "That's the First Rule, and you broke it."

Skink shrugged like he didn't know or care about our Rules. And that's when it hit me—just how different Skink was. He *didn't* know our Rules; he had never heard our Tales. He might look like us, but he really was an outsider.

"According to the Tales," I said, picking my words carefully, "it's our duty to pay respects to humans for what they did for us in the long ago." And I told him the Tale of why the humans had put us here behind the Fence, which is the same Tale I told you before.

Of course, the other monkeys there had heard this all of their lives, and they listened in respectful silence, which was what you were meant to do. But Skink, who was hearing it for the first time, chuckled as I told the Tale, and at the end he actually laughed!

At last, Skink spoke again: "Well, I heard a different story about the very beginning, and you'd better believe there aren't any fences in *this* story."

"Tell us," I said.

"Okay," Skink began. "Well, in the beginning there were *no* animals at all. Not on the land nor in the air, nor even in the sea—nothing. Back then, there was just Father Sky and Mother Earth. . . ."

All the monkeys there were leaning forward to catch every word, and I realized I was doing the same.

"Now, it turned out that Father Sky had a crush on Mother Earth. . . ."

"A crush?" asked some monkey at the front.

"He wanted her to be his wife. So what he did, he made her a gift so that he might win her heart. But this was no ordinary present. It was a living creature, all sleek and silver and shiny.

"But when Father Sky offered his gift, Mother Earth, she just wrinkles her nose and says, 'What is this thing? It smells all . . . fishy.' Now *fishy* wasn't even a word back then, but from that time on, the creature was known as a *fish.* So old Sky just plopped the creature into the ocean, then said to himself, 'What can I do next?'

"Well, Father Sky decided to make a new present. This one was easy to make—it was long and thin, and it didn't have any twiddly bits. He just rolled it out, and when he was done, it was so slithery, he called it a *snake.* But when Mother Earth saw this new gift, she just said, 'Yuck! It's creepy!'

"On and on it went. Father Sky made creature after creature to offer as gifts, but Mother Earth was unimpressed by each and every one. The fly was too dirty, she said, the tortoise too slow, the gorilla too muscle-bound, the cat too vain."

Everyone nodded—we had never seen these animals, but we knew about them from the Tales.

"What about the giraffe?" someone asked.

Skink grinned. "Nope. Neck too long."

"The crocodile?"

"Too toothy."

"How about the dog?"

"Too eager to please. And its breath was too smelly. Well, as you can imagine, Father Sky was getting fed up. Could he ever make a gift that Mother Earth would accept? Then it hit him. He hurried off and made one last animal, which he presented to Mother Earth. 'Hmm,' she says, looking it over. 'It isn't as big as the elephant or as beautiful as the peacock. And it doesn't look as fast as the cheetah or as strong as the bear.' Father Sky says nothing. 'So what does it do?' asks Mother Earth. So Father Sky looks down at the odd little creature, whose name was Sim, and says, 'Do your stuff, kid.'

"And the little monkey—because that's what it was, of course—it begins to jig around and tumble and dance and waggle its bottom and chatter its teeth and scratch its belly and scream and whoop and somersault and wave its tail.

"Mother Earth bursts out laughing at the sight of the creature, and to Father Sky's ears, this laughter is as welcome as rainfall on the desert. At last he had made a gift that won her heart . . . and it was the monkey! And that's how we came to be—all thanks to the first monkey, Sim the Trickster."

I chuckled some, but then this thought hit me— *pow!*—right in my brain.

"What about humans?" I asked.

Skink grinned, like this was a weird question to ask. Then he said, "Well, when he was making the other animals, Father Sky had to throw away all the bits he didn't use. He threw away the snake's legs, and he threw away the fish's ears; he threw away the horse's fingers, and he threw away the turtle's hair. All these leftover bits got jumbled up and stuck together. And one day, they just got up and walked away. And this new creature, which was made up of all those thrown-away parts, decided to call itself *Human*. So it did. And that's why humans look so weird."

There was a gasp of shock from all the monkeys there, including me. Well, it was a shocking thing to say.

"That's not true!" snapped an adult female. "Humans are at the top of the Tree of Life; everyone knows that."

The others murmured agreement, and they were starting to sound all angry and huffy. Skink just smiled.

"What do you know anyway?" said another monkey. Skink kept on smiling.

"I'm getting out of here," declared a Second

Order monkey who I knew had a reputation for not getting angry, only she was looking pretty angry now as she jumped to her feet. The other monkeys did the same.

"You'd better be careful what you say around here," snarled a burly adult over his shoulder.

And then they were gone, the whole muttering pack of them, off into the darkness. Which left just Skink and me.

"That story," I said at last. "You don't believe it, do you?" My voice sounded calm, but inside I was all trembly because I knew that there was another question hidden inside this one, a question I had never dared to ask aloud.

Skink thought it over. "Who knows? Who *cares*? It's just a story—as good as most, and better than some."

"But is it *true*?" I pressed, and then I said it: "Are our Tales wrong?" I felt a tremor of fear at the very act of questioning the Tales that I had been told since I was a baby.

Skink did not reply for some time. Then he said, "Listen, the problem with your Tribe is, you don't know the big picture. You were born inside this Fence of yours, you grew up inside the Fence, it's all you know. You're like some unborn chick, still inside its egg, that sits and wonders what life's all about. But the chick will never find out until it breaks out of the egg—see?"

"I *think* I see." All this talk of chicks and eggs brought an uneasy memory to my mind. "It's like one time, Chim and I were mucking around by the trees and we found this tiny bird's egg. It had fallen from its nest. The shell was smashed to bits and the baby bird was just lying there, all . . . It hadn't even seen anything, it hadn't even gotten out of the egg."

"Ah, well, that's the trick, Kaz, isn't it? You have to make it out of the egg in one piece."

I couldn't see his face in the dark, but I knew that Skink was grinning from ear to ear.

FIVE

THE COUNCIL of Adults met first thing the next morning. The sun had hardly even shown its face, and everything was covered in dew and gray-looking, like all the colors hadn't woken up yet and started going about their business of being colorful. I'd hardly slept—it was nerves about the meeting that stopped me from nodding off, but there was something else, as well. Excitement?

We approached the rocks, Skink, Chim, and I, where the Council waited. In the morning light, they just looked like pale blobs scattered about the rocks. I felt Chim trembling to the left of me, the big wimp. (Of course, I was trembling, too, so that makes me a big wimp as well.) Only Skink seemed relaxed, and maybe that was because he didn't know any better.

We came closer, and every member of the

Council gave us stern looks. Kalibak was sitting on the very highest point, which was called the Great Rock, if you want the official title, and he gave us the sternest look of all. Like I told you, he's the biggest monkey in the whole Tribe, and pretty fierce-looking with it. Up and down he looked at us, down and up, not saying a word. Then at last: "Explain yourselves." And his gaze fell on me first—just my luck. I cleared my throat.

"Well, you see, it all started with this challenge. . . ." I did my best to explain what had happened.

You could tell Kalibak was listening intently, because his brow was all furrowed with concentration. When I was done, he turned to Chim: "Do you have anything to add?"

"No," said Chim in this weird voice that was all high-pitched and squeaky with fear. That's all he said the whole meeting. Next Kalibak turned to Skink.

"And you . . . what explanation do you have for dishonoring a human so?"

Skink grinned, and my heart sank.

"The thing is," he began, "it was just a laugh. . . ." Then, as if to show what he meant, he let out this hooting laugh that you'd never believe Skink's scrawny little frame could hold in the first place. And that's when a thought popped into my mind for the first time, but not for the last: Maybe this new monkey is really crazy?

A few of the Council let out these sharp, disapproving hisses, like *FFSSSSHHHHH!* while others made these scolding *tut-tut* noises. One way or another, it was clear this wasn't the right sort of thing to say, but Skink didn't know or didn't care. Instead, he just made things even worse: "I mean, what are we supposed to do? Honor them? Humans? Give me a break!" He was still smiling, but there was this bitter edge to his voice. I could see anger and outrage spreading throughout the Council. This isn't going well, I thought to myself.

That's when one of the Council members raised his tail, requesting to speak. Kalibak nodded, and Buntu, the Tribe's Wise Monkey, got to his feet. He was our Teller of Tales, an important position, but there was something about him I never trusted. (You know how sometimes you get a grotty old bit of lemon mixed in with the lunchtime feed? Well, that's how Buntu's face looked—like he'd just been sucking on a lemon, all scrunched up and mean.)

"I'm afraid there's more," he said in a voice that was as cold as the dawn air. "I have received reports that this . . . this newcomer has been claiming that the great Tales of long ago are untrue. . . ."

There was another chorus of angry muttering when the Council heard *that.* Buntu pointed a bony finger right at Skink.

"Is this not so?"

Skink just shrugged again, like he couldn't care less.

"These are serious charges," Kalibak declared darkly. The angry grunts around us turned to mutterings of agreement. I felt my heart thudding. I was afraid, but I knew I had to say something.

"Wait!" I cried. "This isn't fair! Skink's only just arrived, he doesn't know the Rules and he's never heard the Tales, but that's not his fault, he shouldn't—"

Kalibak held up a hand, which was his way of saying "Shut up" without actually saying it.

"Enough!" he boomed. "We have all the evidence we need. The Council will reach its decision by sundown. . . ."

And that was that—we were dismissed. We would have to wait the whole day to hear the Council's verdict. I turned to go, giving Chim a tug because he seemed to have forgotten how to work his legs.

That morning I just wanted to be by myself. Too much to think about, I guess. It seemed like my whole world had been turned upside down. I mean, I had grown up knowing nothing except the Tribe and the Council and its Rules . . . but now I kept thinking the Council was being unfair. Could it be that the Rules weren't fair, either? Worse still, was it possible that the Tales weren't completely true? I kept coming back to what Skink had said about the chick inside the egg—how could it know the world from the inside of that shell? Then I remembered how not every bird made it out of the shell alive and kicking. I thought these things over so hard, my brain felt like it was turning to mush or something.

That's when I heard this puffing and panting sound—someone was coming up the tree, but he was taking a long time to do it. At last, a gray head appeared at the foot of my branch. With his face all twisted with the effort of it, Graybak hauled himself up.

"You could always give me a hand, sonny," he panted.

I scooted down the branch and helped him the rest of the way up.

"What's going on?" I asked. It had been ages

since Graybak had climbed a tree—his joints ached too much nowadays.

"I wanted to talk with you in private, Kaz," he said. I knew it was serious when he called me by my real name.

"I heard about the Council meeting this morning. Be careful, Kaz. Kalibak is a strict ruler, and he hates anything that upsets the balance of the Tribe. It isn't smart to go around questioning the Tales."

"But *are* they true?" I blurted. "Are the Tales true?"

Graybak sighed. "Of course they are. You just have to know what you mean by *true,* lad."

This was making my head hurt. "I don't get it."

Graybak's eyes never left mine. "Well . . . Buntu the Teller of Tales would give you a different kind of truth than . . . than the crocodile would, let's say."

For a moment I was lost in thoughts of truth and crocodiles and stuff like that. I shook myself out of it and said, "We'll be okay. I explained to the Council what happened. . . ." I tried to sound upbeat, even though I didn't feel that way.

Graybak shook his head. "You and the boy Chim will be fine—you'll get off lightly. But as for Skink . . . that's a different matter. Kalibak won't stand for a newcomer disrupting things. He might cast him out of the Tribe. That means Skink would be denied food and shelter—it would be against the Rules even to talk with him. Life would be impossible."

"But that's terrible!" I cried, and Graybak's only response was a slow and solemn nod of his head.

"Is there anything we can do?"

Graybak thought my question over. When he did speak again, it seemed as if he'd moved on to a new topic: "I'm an old monkey; my mind plays tricks on me. I just remembered something else about the monkey who escaped all those years ago—the one you keep asking about." I was confused. What did this have to do with anything?

Graybak went on. "When he got back to the Enclosure, he went around saying that there are other places to ride on cars than on the top. Other places to ride . . ." He was smiling this kind of mysterious smile, the sort that makes you wonder what the joke is anyway.

Then the old monkey reached forward and gave me this great big hug, which he had never done before, and I thought I saw his eyes go all watery, but then I felt the wind and I knew that's what had made his eyes water.

After that he rapped me on top of my head with his knuckles and said, "Now start using that brain of yours for once!" And with that, he began to climb back down the tree, leaving me there to wonder what was going on.

It took me a long while to figure things out. Lunch came and went, and I never even bothered to leave the tree to go stuff my face. I ignored the din of the Tribe around me, and I didn't look over to the rocks where the Council was still huddled in debate. I just sat and thought, turning the problem over and over in my mind, until at last I had it. I understood what Graybak had been trying to tell me, and I knew what we could do. For the first time in my life, I felt a step closer to answering one of my Big Questions!

I raced down the tree and began to search the Enclosure.

SIX

THE OTHER monkeys in the Tribe were keeping well away from Skink, as if they thought his troubles might rub off on them if they got too close. I found him sitting on his own, throwing lumps of soil at the sparrows whenever they landed. That was something I'd done a lot of in my time, and I could probably have taught him a thing or two about throwing dirt just right, only my mind was full of other stuff right now. But Skink seemed like he didn't have a care in the world. I squatted down by him and he beamed up at me.

"Hey, Kaz! Thanks for standing up for me like that."

"Yeah, right." I didn't have time for polite conversation. "Listen, you know what we were talking about last night? Well, I think we should do it."

Skink's eyes just danced their merry dance, like he knew what I was going to say. I went on: "There's a chance that the Council will banish you from the Tribe. But it's okay, I've got a plan. . . . We can escape from the Enclosure. You've seen where everything is, so you can guide the way. We'll go to that building, the one with the crocodile—you said you saw where it was. If we can talk to the crocodile . . ." I could hardly believe what I was saying.

Skink raised one eyebrow. It was a question.

"Everyone knows the crocodile is the great historian," I explained. "We can ask *it* about the Tales. If we can prove that the Tales aren't completely true, then how can the Council punish you? And they'll *have* to believe us if we hear it from the crocodile. . . .We'll be doing the Tribe a service. "

"Makes sense." Skink nodded, as if he was agreeing to take a pleasant stroll with an old friend. "Now we just have to figure out how to get over that Fence."

I shook my head. "No, we don't have to go over the Fence at all. . . ." And I explained what Graybak had told me. Skink thought it over a minute, then he threw back his head and let out that great big rolling laugh of his.

"Of course!" he said. "I get it! It's so simple, it's brilliant!" Then he added in a quieter voice, "But I don't think two of us will be enough. We'll need someone else to come. . . ."

It took us a while to find Chim. Usually the little monkey would be up to no good, but today he was just sitting all alone, near a bunch of bushes. The meeting had shaken him.

"Hey, hairball," I said, but he didn't even bother to insult me back. Skink and I sat down.

"Chimmy," I said, all serious, "have I ever made you do anything dumb?"

Chim gave me this suspicious look. "Yeah . . . lots of times."

"Well . . ." I took a deep breath. There was no way to lead in to this, so I just up and said it. "We're going to escape, Skink and I. Break out of the Enclosure. " I tried to sound casual, like it was no big deal.

I could see Chim was stunned. "What do you mean? You can't do that, it's . . . it's against—"

"We're not going to be outside the Fence for long," put in Skink, giving me a sideways glance.

"Just enough time to go see the crocodile. We'll get the answers to some questions, then we'll be back here before anyone knows it. It's the only way we'll be able to convince the Council."

"Come with us," I said. "You won't have to do any of the dangerous stuff."

"No way! I'm not—"

"You're my oldest friend. I never do anything without you."

"It's crazy, just—"

"*Please* . . . We need you. We can't do it with just the two of us."

Chim was quiet for a long while. I knew he thought the whole idea was crazy, but he could tell that I was going to do it anyway. At last he let out this long sigh and said, "Not outside for very long, right?"

We both nodded—right.

Another sigh, and then a quiet "Okay, then." I knew it was the hardest thing Chim had ever done in his life, and he wasn't doing it because he wanted to see what lay beyond the Fence—he was doing it because he was my friend and he wanted to look out for me. I let out a great big whoop of happiness, *WHOOOOOOO-UP!*

And then it was down to business.

We had to wait ages. Every time a car arrived, I'd look over at Skink, who had worked out the details of the plan. But every time, he'd just shake his head no. We were sitting at a bend in the road that was hidden from most of the Enclosure. That had been my idea: I was worried that the Tribe would get suspicious about what we were up to. I needn't have worried—it seemed like everyone was making a point of *not* looking at us.

Right when I was starting to think we would be waiting forever, it came into the Enclosure—a *van,* which is to say, a *car,* only bigger.

"This one!" said Skink.

We watched the van drive through the Enclosure. It pulled up not too far from us, and we made our move. The Rules were pretty clear about where you could go on any car or van. The top parts were fine, but underneath was strictly forbidden. Still, we were past worrying about the Rules now. We looked around quickly to make sure no one was watching; then we scampered right underneath the van. It was dark down there, and we had to crawl on our bellies to stop from clunking our heads.

"Careful," Skink warned us. "Don't touch the hot parts!"

He pointed to something near the inside of a wheel and said that was the part we should grab. There was one near each wheel—Skink took up position at one of the front ones, and Chim went opposite him. I scooted down to the back end and took a firm grip on the thing with my arms and legs.

"Make sure your tail doesn't hang out," shouted Skink. "We can't let anyone see us."

It was cramped and noisy under there, and I wasn't sorry when we started moving. Everything started rumbling and shaking and juddering like crazy. When I looked down, I could see the ground rushing beneath me, so that it was all blurred. It looked weird, but then I looked up and saw something even weirder—another monkey hanging on near the wheel opposite mine. Blok!

The big monkey was glaring at me fit to bust. "You and your little friends aren't getting the better of me again!" he shouted over the rumble of the van. There wasn't much to say to that, so I didn't say anything. I just watched the ground whiz by.

After a while, the van slowed down again, then stopped, and I knew it had come to the building at the edge of the Fence, where the Guards sit and keep watch. I heard the crunch of a Guard's steps on the road beside my wheel. . . . I felt this stab of fear—surely they would find us—but then the van began to move again. For a few seconds, the shaking got worse than ever, so bad that it was all I could do to hold on tight. I knew that we must be crossing the grille that lay across the gap in the Fence, and that thought helped me keep my grip. Then the bumping died down again and I realized we had done it—we had left the Enclosure. Outside the Fence! I could feel the excitement hammering in my heart.

I heard Skink's shout over the noise of the van: "Now!" The plan was to jump before the van picked up too much speed. I took a deep breath and let go. Skink had warned us to roll inward toward the center of the van and lie flat. He said that if we tried to go the other way, we might get splatted by the wheels. I hit the ground and rolled flat. I blinked my eyes and saw sky above, light all around me again. The van was rumbling off down the road, away from us.

The other three monkeys were on the road, too, all looking dazed.

Chim stared at Blok in amazement. "What are *you* doing here?"

But Skink snapped, "No time for that now—we've got to move!"

It was true. We were in the open ground between our Enclosure and that of the lions. If any of the Guards looked this way, it would be no big trick to spot us. But we were lucky—no Guard *did* look our way, and we were able to scurry over to the tree by the road and shinny up it.

Once we were inside its branches, we knew we were safe. Skink gave this odd chuckle deep in his throat; then he looked at Blok. "So what *are* you doing here?"

"If something's going on, I want to be in on it," Blok said. His lip curled into a snarl. "You're not going to show me up a second time."

"That's okay," I said, "but we can't fight among ourselves—we're going to have to look out for one another."

We quickly told Blok the plan, and he did a good job of still looking tough when he heard it. Then I held out my hand. The others knew what I meant. Chim placed his hand on top of mine first, and I noticed it was all trembly and shaky. Then Skink put his hand on top of Chim's, and finally Blok put *his* meaty fist on top of Skink's.

"It's settled, then," I said. Everyone nodded very slowly and solemnly, as was only fitting for a time like this.

"What now?" asked Chim.

Skink leaned back against a branch and wriggled down till he got good and comfy. "Now we wait."

So that's what we did.

We sat as still as we could. The excitement of being on the other side of the Fence was beginning to wear off a bit—after all, I had spent practically every day of my life sitting in a tree. But then something happened. One of the Guards' trucks drove up and stopped right underneath us. Two Guards got out and leaned against the truck. They each drank something brown and murky out of these little white things they held.

One of them started talking, and it sounded like "Blahblahblahblahblahblahblah."

And then the other one, in this deeper voice, went, "Blahblahblahblahblah."

And so on. I couldn't understand a word. The thing is, of all the animals in the world, humans are the only kind that turned their back on the One True Tongue that we all speak—every single animal, big or small, furry or scaled. Humans are the only animal that we can't understand, not a single word, and, in return, they can't understand a word we say. According to the Tales, the reason why they rejected the One True Tongue was this:

Human was walking through the World Forest one day when it came across a box. Now that box contained some very special knowledge— the Knowledge of Machines, to be precise. Human was eager to learn the secret of wheels and cogs and Electricity, and it tore open the box right away and took that knowledge greedily. It learned many incredible things, but there was a price to pay. For ever since that day, humans have been unable to communicate with the rest of the animals . . . and now they have forgotten that they ever could. . . .

Anyway, there we were, listening to the mysterious chatter of the two Guards below, when Skink suddenly whispered, "I wish they'd shut up. What a stupid conversation!"

I was amazed. "You can understand humans?"

"Sure." He shrugged like it was no big deal. "Not that I ever heard one say anything worth hearing."

"Where did you learn that?" asked Chim. Just from the way he said it, I could tell Chim didn't believe him.

"Here and there," answered Skink. "I've picked up a lot of things. . . ."

"So what are they talking about now, then?" challenged Blok.

Skink cocked his head and listened for a moment; then he said, "Not much—what they saw last night on something called *television,* which is a moving-pictures box that humans sit and watch for hour after hour. They were watching something called *football,* which is just a bunch of oversized humans with nothing better to do than gallumph around after something called a *ball.*"

"You don't like humans much, do you?" I asked.

Skink gave no reply. Instead he said, "We'll have to wait until it's getting dark—when no more humans are visiting and the Guards are busy getting everything ready for night. Then we'll have to cut south across the lion enclosure."

Chim shook his head and stuck one finger in his ear. "Sorry—for a moment, I thought you said *lion* enclosure."

"It's the only way," said Skink with a grin. "But

don't worry—we'll be in and out before the big cats even know what's happening. And then . . ."

"And then on to the crocodile," I said.

"Yeah, right."

Chim was shaking his head. "I don't like this—I don't like this one little bit."

But he knew it was too late to turn back—if he gave himself up, we would all be caught. So he just buried his little head in his knees and went on saying, "I don't like this. I don't like this, nope, I don't. . . ."

I reached over and gave his tail a friendly tug. Then we sat and waited for darkness.

SEVEN

IT TAKES ages for the sky to get dark when you've got nothing to do but watch it second by second and will the sun to go away. But gradually the sky did darken to purple and we saw the first stars twinkling through a gap in the clouds.

"At least the stars are watching over us," said Chim.

He didn't mean anything by it, but Skink snapped, "What is that supposed to mean?"

Chim shrugged. "The stars—you know, they watch over us when we're sleeping. Well, okay, I know we're not sleeping, but they can still watch over us, can't they?"

"It's in the Tales," growled Blok.

I didn't know why this got Skink so riled up. He wouldn't let go. "And what else do the Tales say?

Why doesn't the sky just stay blue and let us watch out for ourselves, eh?"

"Well, it goes dark to help us sleep better," said Chim. "According to the Tales."

Skink made a kind of *PFAH!* "I'll tell you why the sky is dark at night," he said.

"Why?" (That was me.)

Skink's grin was triumphant. "No reason at all! That's just the way it is. Look up and you see darkness that goes on and on. The tale is that there's no tale. Get it?"

The fact is, I *didn't*—get the joke, I mean, if that's what it was. I didn't want to think about it, either. "The crocodile," I murmured. "The crocodile will know. . . ."

Skink looked like he was about to say something, but then he caught himself and just nodded. The conversation died out to silence, and I was glad— gladder still when it was finally dark enough for us to head out.

We shinnied down the tree and set off. It felt good to be on the move again. There were no Guards that I could see near us. Skink led the way, and even Blok didn't kick up a stink about that. The big monkey was acting all tough, same as ever, but the act wasn't working too well. I could tell that he was as scared as the rest of us.

The fence around the lions' enclosure was different from the Fence—by which I mean *our* Fence. (The funny thing is, once you had crossed it, it seemed weird to be saying *the* Fence. I was starting to think of the Fence as just one among many. Same with the Enclosure.) Anyway, the lions' fence was thicker and stronger-looking, and it did not have the power of Electricity running through it. It was built for much bigger animals, which meant the gaps were wide enough for us monkeys to slip through easily, so that's what we did. We began to scurry across the open ground, keeping our heads down and trying not to make any noise.

A weird picture popped into my mind of what we must look like—four little monkeys creeping along while the pride of lions lazed around not far upwind of us. How many times had I heard the roar of those lions from inside the safety of our Fence? I'd never expected to be on the wrong side of *their* fence. It gave me this horrible shivery feeling just thinking about it, but I couldn't help thinking about it. We plodded on, picking our way carefully because we didn't know this ground at all.

"If we stick over on this side of the enclosure," hissed Skink, "we should be okay."

He sounded so confident that I almost believed him, and everything *was* okay . . . for about two minutes. We had made it to halfway across the enclosure, when—*RRRRAAAARRRRGGHHH!*—this huge roar boomed out. It sounded like it was ripping a hole in the night, if you know what I mean. I almost jumped out of my monkey skin.

"No big deal," said Skink, still moving, head down. "Lions just like to make a lot of noise, that's all."

But the roar sounded again, and this time it was even louder. That meant it was closer. *Much* closer.

When I remember what happened next, it seems like everything was in slow motion. Someone yelled, "Run!" I think it was Skink. The four of us took off, and we all went in different directions. The next instant, I was all alone, charging through the tall grass with no idea where I was headed. I was running as fast as I could, but it felt like I was hardly moving, as if I was running underwater or something.

I heard that roar again—this time so loud, it seemed to fill the whole sky, and then echo around inside my brain until there was nothing left in there but terror. I glimpsed something out of the corner of my eye. I couldn't make it out, but two things were clear: It was big and it was fast. No, make that three things: It was big, it was fast, and it was coming my way.

I didn't think—no time to think—my instincts took over. I changed directions, zigzagged through the tall grass toward the shrubbery. If I could just make it to the trees beyond . . . I heard this dreadful sound behind me, like something powerful *was* racing through the grass, and that was because something powerful was racing through the grass, and my heart was hammering at superspeed, but the trees were getting closer, now if I could just—

Something sharp and powerful and *big* gripped me by the back of the neck and swept me up off my feet, clean off the ground. *What the . . .* My legs dangled. It was a lion, had to be! A lion was holding me in its mighty jaws, with its mighty teeth, and I was feeling mighty terrified. Its breath, all hot and angry, blew against the back of my head. I tried to cry out, but my brain had shut down, what with being totally terrified and all, and I couldn't find any words.

The beast that held me in its jaws began to pad back through the long grass. Another big cat appeared in front of us. Even in my terror, a memory floated back to me: Graybak had told me that it was the lionesses who did all the hunting. Certainly the giant animal in front of me lacked the telltale mane of the male of the species. The lioness moved her gigantic head close to me to get a better look, and I remember thinking that a mouth as big as that could swallow me whole, no problem. When she spoke, I got a good view of her enormous yellowish fangs.

"Good work, Cynthia," she said to the one holding me, who was not able to speak because she had a mouthful of something—namely, me. Instead she nodded her head, which gave me a good bone shaking. The other lioness fixed me with big yellow-brown eyes. When I looked into those eyes, I saw only one message and it said, "Uh-oh, you're in trouble now, Kaz."

"Tricky little rascal," declared the lioness. "Almost made it to the trees, didn't you?" She turned her attention back to Cynthia. "We'd better get this little whippersnapper back to the pride."

They began to canter down the length of their enclosure, toward where the pride hung out. The cool night air rushed against me, but that wasn't why

I was trembling. I was trembling because I knew I was about to be eaten.

At last we got there, and I was dropped on the ground, right next to a couple of piles of soggy leaves. I looked again and saw it wasn't two piles of soggy leaves—it was Chim and Blok. They looked like I felt, which is to say, they looked wide-eyed with terror. You couldn't blame them. We were surrounded by about twenty lions, all licking their great big chops like we were the tastiest snack food going. I had no idea where Skink was—perhaps he'd made it to the trees?

"Well, well, well," Cynthia said, able to speak again. "What have we here?"

"Supper!" hollered one of the lion cubs, and a few of the younger cats chuckled.

"That *is* our normal policy," chipped in a scrawny lion. "Trespassers will be eaten."

"Not much meat on them, though," grumbled another.

"Find out what they're doing here first, Agnes," an elderly lioness called.

The lioness who had addressed me earlier turned her great big head toward us now. "That's a point," she said. "What are you doing here?"

I knew Chim and Blok were no use. I would have to answer.

"We're going to see the crocodile," I said. "We . . . er . . . we want to ask it some questions. . . ." The words sounded stupid to me as soon as I spoke them. The whole trip sounded stupid. It suddenly didn't seem so important, and I wished I was back in the safety of the trees, on the right side of our Fence— the *inside*.

"What *is* it going on about?" roared one lion. Then to me: "Stop mumbling, monkey!"

"I say eat 'em," said another. "Ask questions later."

"Yeah, eat 'em," growled yet another. "It's not as though we get to hunt our supper down every day, is it?"

"Hear! Hear!"

It seemed like the decision was made—suppertime, and we were on the menu. But suddenly a great deep voice roared out and made everyone freeze. What it said was, "Hold on!"

The whole pride turned to look, and so did we. It was a lion, but not just any lion. This one was *huge*— the biggest of the pride by far. It padded up slowly, and I realized that something was standing up high on the back of its neck, gripping on to the great beast's shaggy mane. Skink!

The little monkey was actually riding the leader of the pride! My bottom jaw probably fell to the ground in amazement. Just at that moment, the full moon popped out from behind a cloud. It lit up the nighttime sky right behind Skink's head, so that he was framed against it—the skinny little monkey riding the mighty lion! I saw the flash of teeth as Skink grinned.

"Charles . . . what on *earth* is going on?" It was the lioness in charge, Agnes. She didn't sound happy.

The big lion, the one called Charles, lowered his head so that Skink could jump off. The little monkey did so with a nifty front somersault with a half twist.

"Look what I found, darling," Charles said. His voice was deep and booming, but not the brightest-sounding, to tell you the truth. "Got this little fella scampering across the enclosure. Bagged him near the trees. . . ."

"Yes . . . and?" The lioness sounded like she was trying to be patient, but it took a lot of effort.

"And . . . well, listen to what the little fella has to say, Agnes. . . ."

Skink took his cue. He raised himself to his full

height, which wasn't much in the middle of all those giant cats, and said, "Well, I was just telling the big guy here what I thought everyone knew. I'm surprised you'd never heard it before."

"Heard what?" snapped Agnes.

"That all the other animals know the lion as 'King of the Beasts,'" said Skink with a pleasant smile. "I mean, that's your proper, official title." The monkey looked back at the giant lion. "Isn't that right, Your Majesty?"

Charles seemed to swell even larger with pride. (That's *pride* in the sense of being proud, not *pride* in the sense of a bunch of lions, if you see what I mean.)

"Well," said the lion, "now that you mention it . . . I *have* always felt there was something . . . ahem . . . *regal* about us—a cut above the common animals."

"You got that right," agreed Skink.

I could tell that the rest of the pride had no objections to the idea, either—like it was nice to get a little well-deserved recognition from the rest of the animal kingdom.

"King of the Beasts, you say?" asked one, licking its paws.

"That's right." Skink nodded. "Or sometimes you

hear 'King of the Jungle,' or 'King of the Animals,' if you're not keen on the word *beasts.*"

"I don't mind *beasts,*" commented one lion. "Sounds rather rugged."

"Rugged is good."

"It works for me."

"Then it's decided," announced Charles. "King of the Beasts it is!"

Agnes let out a sharp breath—*hufffff!* or something like that—which I took to mean that she thought this was a load of old nonsense. But the others seemed pretty pleased, especially the male lions.

A sudden thought struck one of the pride. "But what about the humans?"

"What *about* them?" answered Skink, his smile never wavering. "They bring you food every day, don't they? Just serving the King of the Beasts, as is only proper."

The pride nodded happily at this—it made perfect sense to their feline brains.

"Now, Your Majesties, if I can be so bold," continued Skink, "may we ask you to make your first royal decision?"

Charles nodded his great big shaggy head in this new way he probably thought looked regal—

sort of slow and dignified.

"We request safe passage through your enclosure," said Skink.

Charles thought it over in a kingly manner. "A good sovereign must show mercy as well as strength," he said in a new voice, all high-and-mighty-sounding. "Greatness does not come from eating pip-squeaks such as you. . . . Your request is granted."

Skink made a big over-the-top bow, and I reckon I was the only one who saw the glint in his eye as he did it—all sparkly and mischievous, like he was having fun! Maybe he *is* crazy, I thought.

But you had to hand it to him—Skink had stopped us from being eaten. What's more, as was only fitting their new regal generosity, the lions insisted on giving us an escort to the far side of their enclosure. But this time I wasn't carried in a lion's jaws. No, this time I rode on the lion's back. With the darkness rushing against me, and the mighty muscles of the big cat working beneath me as I gripped its fur—just for that instant I forgot my fear and had this amazing feeling of freedom and power that I had never known before.

It didn't last long, though. The lions soon

reached the far boundary of their enclosure and dropped us off. Blok and Chim were still looking a bit stunned by everything, but Skink was beaming. Me, I wasn't sure how I felt—lots of different feelings were jostling in my brain, making it impossible to identify any one of them.

Just before the lions turned to go, the lioness named Agnes hung her head low so it was right near mine. It seemed like she was staring right through me. "You were lucky, little monkey. Lucky Charles got in on the act," she said in this soft murmur. "*We* would have eaten you. . . ." Looking into those hunter's eyes, I didn't doubt it, not for an instant.

Then they turned and ran back—a jumble of pale shapes disappearing into the darkness.

Skink clapped his hands together. "Time to move on."

EIGHT

IT WAS pretty dark now and there wasn't much chance of being spotted, so we trotted along down the road. At one point a truck drove by, but we just hid behind a line of bushes and it never even slowed down. The Guards were too busy getting all the big animals into their sleeping quarters for the night.

Back on the road, I made a point of running alongside Skink. "That was incredible," I said. "With the lions."

Skink's teeth flashed in the gloom. "Most animals are happy, if you just tell 'em what they want to hear. Doesn't matter if it's true or not."

"You mean it *isn't* true about them being called King of the Beasts?"

The little monkey stuck out his bottom lip. "Depends. I mean, I've heard people use the expression before about lions. But do I believe it? Well, consider this—if they're so regal, why are they on the *inside* of a fence, just like us? How regal does that sound to you?"

It was a tough question and I was flat out of answers, so I just fell in line with Chim and Blok. On we ran. Finally we came to this place where the road split in two. Skink looked both ways and scratched his head.

"Now, which way was it?" he murmured.

A pang of panic did a little hop, skip, and jump in my gut.

"You can't remember?" I asked.

Skink didn't reply, just set off running toward the left. We followed, and for a while the only sound was the panting of our breath and the scratch of our feet on the road. We were approaching a low building. On a tree in front of it I could make out some dark jagged shapes. As we got closer, I saw what they were. Three of them—great big ugly birds—were lined up on a gnarled old branch. Their shoulders arched high above their long, skinny necks and bald heads.

They didn't move a feather as we approached.

"What are *they*?" Blok asked, and his voice was kind of edgy, like he didn't know what to expect next. So much for Blok the tough guy, I thought.

"No big deal," replied Skink. "They're just vultures."

"They look hungry," said Chim unhappily, and, true enough, the three birds were eyeing us with this peckish glint in their beady eyes.

"Don't worry, we're not their kind of meal," said Skink. "We're too alive." Then the little monkey scuttled up to the birds and raised a hand. "Evening, all. How's things?"

"Oh, same old thing," answered a vulture in this flat, deadpan way it had of talking. "It's *dead* exciting around here." The other two vultures chuckled a dark chuckle—sort of *huh, huh, huh*—and I once again couldn't figure out the joke.

"What are you all doing here in the *dead* of night?" asked another vulture, also in a flat voice. Hey? It wasn't the dead of night, but the third vulture burst out into more chuckles at this comment.

"SSSHHH," said the first vulture. "You laugh loud enough to wake the *dead.*"

This set all three of them off again—*huh, huh, huh*—which made their sinister-looking shoulders and wings jiggle up and down. It was creepy.

"What's going on?" I asked Skink out of the side of my mouth, never taking my eyes off the vultures.

The little monkey shrugged. "Just vultures being vultures," he said, like that made everything clear. "See, they're scavengers—they only eat animals that are already dead."

"Yuck!" exclaimed Chim, screwing up his nose. "That's disgusting!"

"Not really," I said. "I mean, at least they don't kill anything. They just eat up leftovers."

"That's right," said Skink. "The only thing is, their sense of humor is a bit on the . . . dark side."

He could say that again. These vultures laughed at any mention of death and dying, which is not a very funny topic according to most monkeys (me included). I guess what they say is true: It takes all sorts of animals to make a world.

When their chuckles had died down, Skink tried again.

"We're looking for the crocodile," he said. "Which way do we need to go?"

One of the vultures nodded its head to the left. "Carry on *dead* straight in that direction," it said. "You'll come to a crossroads. The reptile house is right in front of you, *dead* center." The other two vultures continued to chuckle at each mention of the word *dead.*

"Got it." Skink nodded. He didn't seem fazed. "Thanks a lot—you've been *dead* helpful," he said with a wink.

This set the vultures off laughing again. To be honest, all this chuckling was getting me down, and I was keen to leave these gruesome birds behind. But first I had to know something.

"You're not inside any kind of fence. Why don't you all just fly away?"

"We can't fly anywhere. The humans have pulled out one big feather from each of our wings."

"Doesn't that hurt?"

Three pair of giant hooded shoulders shrugged. "Makes you feel like *death* warmed over," said one bird.

It was as good a way to end the conversation as any. We monkeys ran off, but I could still hear that low, dark sound, *huh, huh, huh,* and it kept rattling around my skull even when I was sure the birds were too far away to be heard.

At last we came to a cluster of low buildings. There were signs with those squiggles on them, which is to say, more of that writing stuff humans go in for so much. But there were pictures on these signs as well. You know pictures—things that sort of looked like animals but weren't real animals. These pictures were just flat shapes, like when you make a face in the dirt with your finger. One had the outline of a lizard on it. "Here it is!" said Skink. "The reptile house."

"How come they get to live in one of these building places?" asked Chim.

Skink was looking for a way in. "Well," he said, "the reptiles can't be outside here. The temperature has to be kept good and hot for them."

"So what now?" panted Blok, who might have been big and strong but wasn't used to so much running.

"Now we get in," said Skink. He pointed to a spot high on the side of the building. "Through that window."

Blok stared upward. "Oh yeah?" he asked. "How?" I didn't much like agreeing with Blok, but he had a point. There was nothing we could grip to climb up there.

Skink grinned. "Funny you should ask. . . ."

So this is how we did it. Skink told us all what to do. First Blok stood at the bottom, being the biggest. Then I climbed up and stood on his shoulders. We were pretty wobbly, but we steadied ourselves against the building. "You okay?" I asked Blok, and he said, "Gnnnngh," which I think meant yes. Then Skink made Chim stand in front of us, and the little monkey had to cup his hands together.

When Skink was happy with the way we looked, he walked away. I thought he might keep on walking, but at last he stopped, turned, and started charging toward us. When he had picked up enough speed, he leapt up into the air. One of his feet landed in Chim's hands, and Chimmy shoved upward with all his strength. Skink sprang higher still, and one of his feet landed in my cupped hands. I shoved upward with all my strength, and Skink shot up toward the window. He only just caught the ledge with his fingers, but it was enough. He hauled himself up the rest of the way, then disappeared through the window. He was in! I hopped down off Blok's shoulders, and then we waited.

It wasn't long before a door in the front of the building opened, and Skink's smiling face appeared through the crack.

"Where did you learn to do that?" I asked.

"A place called the *circus,*" he said. I didn't even bother asking what that was—I'd learned by now that Skink didn't like discussing the past too much.

"And now . . . come this way," he said.

NINE

IT WAS weird being inside a human building—looking up and not seeing branches or sky overhead, just this low, flat thing called the *ceiling*. It was dark in there, and a strange kind of stillness hung in the air. I wished I could feel a breeze on my face. We crept along, with Skink leading the way.

A row of darkened windows slid by on our right. You couldn't see much in the shadows on the other side of them, and in a way I was glad. I kept as far from them as I could, but Skink pressed his face to each window and peered inside.

"Is that it?" I kept asking, but Skink just shook his head.

But then: "This is the one we want."

We had stopped outside a much bigger window. I

looked in, and though I couldn't see anything in the murky gloom, something about it gave me the creeps big time. Maybe this wasn't such a good idea after all. But we had come so far. I knew we couldn't turn back, not now.

"So how do we get in?" I asked.

No answer—Skink was busy running his fingers across the wall.

"What are you looking for?"

"This," he said. He tapped the wall, and it made a kind of rattling sound. "It's a *panel.* See, they probably use it to put food in there or something."

I ran my fingers over the same area. I could feel the straight edges of the thing Skink was talking about, but I didn't see what good it was. It was firmly shut. "Okay," I said, "but how are we going to get in?"

That's when Blok stepped up, and for the first time since we had been outside the Fence, he seemed like his old self—big, dumb, swaggering Blok.

"Step aside, wimps," he said in a snarl that sounded like he'd been practicing it.

Blok gave the panel a couple of whacks with his fists to test it out; then he really got down to business, driving his shoulder against the panel with all his might. He threw back his head with the effort and let out these grunting sounds, but when I tried to help, he shook his head no. It was like it was a personal challenge for him—to accept help would be to admit defeat. That's how Blok's brain worked, so I just let him get on with it.

But Blok was a very strong monkey, no doubt about it, and at last the panel started to show signs of loosening. "C'mon, you big lunk!" Skink shouted. "You can do it!"

There was this huge cracking sound, and then the panel swung inward—in to where the crocodile waited.

"Good job," said Skink, and he gave Blok a pat on the head like he was a baby just off his mother's back or something. Blok grunted. The little monkey stepped into the opening. He had a quick look at the panel door, then said, "Someone'll have to hold it open. If it swings shut, I don't think we'll be able to open it again from the inside."

We hadn't discussed what would happen now, but it was clear to me what had to be done—after all, I had talked Chim into coming, and Blok hadn't known what he was letting himself in for. So I said, "I'll go in with Skink. You two wait at the door. Blok, you hold it open, okay?"

So in we went. There was some kind of heater set

into the low ceiling, and it gave off a weird red light, so that everything had this red tint to it, but at least you could see. The room was low and square. On one side, there were a few rocks and some bushes; the rest of the room was taken up by a big pool of water. There was a big old log lying in the water, but no signs of a crocodile. Where could it be?

I looked back—Chim was standing just inside of the door. I wasn't sure if he was curious or afraid to stand outside in the dark on his own. Blok was holding the panel open with one muscled arm. The gravel crunched under my feet.

"What now?" I whispered. Skink pointed a single finger out to the pool.

The log didn't move, not once, but with a shock I realized that it wasn't a log at all—it was the crocodile, and it was watching us with these beady yellow eyes that broke just above the surface of the water. I was pretty terrified, to tell you the truth, but I hadn't come so far to leave without answers. I forced my legs to go a little closer. The crocodile was lying completely still—*dead* still, as the vultures would say—and the tip of its nose was above the water's surface as well. The Tales had not done the crocodile justice. I could see the armor-plated ridges of its back and its mighty tail. I had this horrible feeling that the lions had been a doddle compared with this—no amount of smooth talking would help us here. We were looking at a killing machine, plain and simple.

Suddenly the crocodile raised its head up out of the water and treated us to a welcoming smile. At least it was meant to be a welcoming smile, but it didn't feel very welcoming, not with so many teeth on display, all stacked up in neat and deadly rows.

"Well, well, well . . . visitors," said the crocodile in a quiet voice that made me shiver on the inside. "No one has ever come to see me before—not *inside* this cage at least."

Of course, Skink made the first move. "We're here to ask you some questions," he said.

"About us," I added. "About ourselves, I mean."

"Ah," said the crocodile. "My reputation as a historian precedes me. Come closer now, little monkeys; I won't bite. They feed me adequately in here."

We moved closer, but not too close. I still hung way back from the water. Skink was right up near its edge—wasn't he even a tiny bit afraid? If he was, he didn't show it.

"My friend here"—Skink nodded toward me—"my friend wants to know how his tribe came to be in this place—inside their enclosure, that is." And he quickly told the crocodile our Tale of how we came to be inside the Fence.

"We want to know if it's true," I added.

Incredibly, the crocodile's smile widened, and he glided ever so slightly closer. "Well, like most tales, it is *partly* true. Just like my own kind, you monkeys are not originally from here."

"Where *are* we from?"

"Oh, lots of places, and all of them far, far away. It's true that humans brought you here, but it was really not so very long ago . . . and their motives were not entirely to protect you." Was it my imagination, or was the crocodile closer now? His legs didn't seem to be moving or his tail swishing in the water, but I couldn't help thinking that, little by little, he was getting nearer. But I couldn't stop yet. I had to know more.

"Why did they bring us?" I asked.

"Any number of reasons," answered the crocodile sweetly. "Don't expect an easy explanation for anything humans do. Why, just a few decades ago, there was a craze among them to wear monkey-fur coats. Almost a million of your comrades were killed in the name of something known as *fashion*. . . ."

I couldn't help shuddering at the thought. "That's gross!" exclaimed Chim from way at the back of the room, near the panel door that Blok held open.

"Not monkeys like you, I hasten to add," the crocodile said. "Your fur is far too . . . homely. Believe me, you'd be surprised at how many shapes and sizes of monkey there are in the world. And then, of course, we can't forget your grander relatives—the gorilla, the orangutan, the dear old chimpanzee. . . . Not exactly monkeys, but part of the family."

Chimpanzee, gorilla, orangutan. I had heard these names in the Tales, but nothing more. What did the crocodile mean? The reptile sensed my bewilderment. "The so-called great apes?" it prompted. "Though, of course, greatness is in the eye of the beholder. I should think the lesser apes are furious."

The crocodile chuckled as if it found what it was saying wonderfully amusing. Good that someone did, I suppose.

"So why are *we* here?" I asked. "Why is the Tribe in the Enclosure? In this place?"

"Entertainment, mostly. Of course, your kind are not all kept in places like this. There are lots of different forms of entertainment. The humans find you . . . amusing, and so they have you perform in circuses"—I threw a quick glance at Skink, who was staring straight ahead at the crocodile—"or sometimes they even keep you as pets. And of course they put you in places like this—prisons called *zoos* and *wildlife parks,* where they can come and have a good look and a giggle, and then they can go back home to the world of humans and never give you a second thought."

I felt some tears trying to squeeze their way out of my eyeballs, so I blinked them back quickly. This was terrible! I had come looking for the truth, but not this. I looked over at Skink, who was giving me this weird look, like . . . I don't know, like he wished I wasn't there. Neither of us noticed that the crocodile had moved closer still, and his great big jaws were only a few feet from where Skink crouched.

"Of course," purred the crocodile (and there was almost a kind of hypnotic quality to that gentle voice), "there is another important point to remember about you monkeys, another purpose you can serve. . . ."

It all happened in an instant. One moment, the crocodile was flat and still in the water. The next moment, the reptile bellowed "FOOD!" and then it was leaping through the air and its gigantic mouth, full of razor-sharp choppers, was opening wide to grab Skink and eat him alive. The crocodile was fast, but Skink was faster. He leapt up high, and the crocodile's jaws snapped shut on air and nothing else, making a horrible sound, sort of *CLAKKK!*

But Skink wasn't out of danger yet—oh no. The crocodile swung its head up and whacked the little monkey, still in midair, backward, so that he went into the water with a plopping sound. Skink went right under the surface and he didn't come up again. The crocodile let out this terrible hissing sound and wheeled around, then slid back into the water of the pool to find Skink. The crocodile's mighty tail swished back and forth, and then the giant reptile disappeared under the surface, too, so all I could see was this great big black shape underwater.

I heard a shout from behind me: "No!" It was Chim, his voice pulled tight with fear. I looked around and saw my friend looking all helpless and panicky and *alone*. Blok was gone, and the panel that he had been holding open had swung shut. He had left us! Chim was tugging frantically at the panel door, letting out loads of squeaks and grunts as he tried to open it. I scurried over and tried to help. I yanked on the thing so hard, I could feel my eyeballs bulging and almost popping out with the strain, but it was no good. The door would not budge, you could only open it from the other side. "Blok!" I shouted at the top of my voice. "Come back!" But there was no reply from the other side, and I knew the big, dim monkey had run away.

I turned back around and looked at the pool. Neither Skink nor the crocodile had surfaced. I knew from the Tales that the fearsome crocodile wouldn't have any problem staying underwater, but Skink? The little monkey couldn't hold his breath so long . . . could he? Surely the crocodile must have him by now? And then it would be our turn.

Suddenly the crocodile burst up out of the pool, and water sloshed all over the place. But the crocodile's mouth was closed, and I could see why—Skink had wrapped his entire body around the tip of the giant reptile's snout. The crocodile *couldn't* open its jaws. It splashed down into the water and then swung up again, shaking its head and trying to get rid of the pesky monkey clinging to it. That's when I heard Skink's shout, but he wasn't shouting "Help!" and he wasn't screaming in terror or anything like that. What Skink shouted was "Yeeee-hah!"—like he was having a blast—and that thought popped into my brain again: He's crazy. He's really, really crazy. . . . The crocodile went on thrashing around in the pool, and water was flying everywhere, but Skink held tight.

That's when I spotted it—a grille on the far side of the room, beyond the pool. It was smaller than the panel door we had come in by, but it looked big enough. We might just be able to get out that way! "Come on!" I yelled to Chim, but he couldn't even move, he was so afraid. I grabbed his arm and tugged him along. We raced around the pool, with water spraying and splashing all over us, and made it to the grille.

We grabbed hold of it and pulled like we'd never pulled before. "It's not going to come," gasped Chim, but he was wrong, I felt it loosen just a little, now if we could only . . . The crocodile's deadly tail loomed up out of the water and swept toward us. I jumped up out of the way just in time, and it whizzed by under my feet. Chim wasn't so lucky. The tail caught him—*WHUMP!*—and knocked him sideways into the wall. I rushed back to the grille and, using every last bit of strength I had, yanked one last time. It came free in my hands! There was a little tunnel beyond. We could escape!

"Let's go!" I shouted. I helped Chim to his feet and began to push him into the narrow darkness of that tunnel. His tail waggled out and I tucked it in behind him, then I clambered in as well. I turned back and shouted, "Skink!" The crazy little monkey was still riding the giant crocodile, one arm waving free in the air. He looked over my way and grinned, and I saw this wild gleam in his eye. Then he let go of the crocodile's snout. Immediately the reptile opened up its great jaws, and I saw all those jagged teeth again, but it was too late now, because Skink was charging along the length of the crocodile's back and hooting with laughter! He jumped off and hit the ground running, ducking under the crocodile's tail as it sliced through the air like a deadly weapon, which it was.

Skink made it to the entrance of the tunnel. I held out my hand for him to grab and said, "Quick!" but Skink just grinned. "What's the rush?" he said. The crocodile was climbing out of the pool, but Skink stayed put. He even began to shimmy and dance about, singing that nutty little tune of his. All the while the crocodile was coming closer and closer, and Skink just kept on jigging and hopping around, even though the reptile was almost upon him, and those enormous jaws were opening up again, so we could see the pink insides of its great big mouth and *teeth,* all those teeth—

Right at the very last moment (and I mean the *very* last moment), Skink hopped up into the safety of the tunnel. "Sorry, monkey's not on the menu tonight," he yelled, and he topped it off with one of those nutty giggles of his. And then we were pushing our way through the pitch-black tunnel, and all I could hear was this angry roar behind us as the crocodile realized his supper had scarpered.

And then, blackness. It seemed like we were crawling in darkness for ages, and I started to think the tunnel would go on and on without end . . . but then I ran straight into Chim's back. He had stopped.

"What is it?" I asked.

"It's come to an end," said Chim, and in the cramped darkness his voice sounded very, very small.

"Let's have a look," I said. I squeezed past him. The tunnel *had* come to an end, but it seemed like there was another kind of panel there. I shoved against it with my shoulder. This one opened quite easily. It fell out with a clatter, and cool air hit me in the face.

I hopped out and looked around. It was good to be outside again, but outside where? We were on the other side of the low buildings. Everything was lit, but not with the light of the moon—there were several of these tall, thin things with orange glows on top of them, and they lit up the place pretty well.

"What are those?" I asked Skink.

"They're lampposts," he said.

"So where are we?" I asked.

"Isn't it obvious?" He pointed to a darkened gate at the far end of the buildings. "That gate is the way in to all of the enclosures, but we're outside it. We're *outside* the zoo."

There was that word again—the one the crocodile had used: *zoo.*

"You mean what the crocodile said . . . it was all true?"

Skink gave a little nod, but he wouldn't look me in the eye.

Before I could say anything else, there was a sudden noise behind us. I whirled round just as a human came out of one of the buildings. It was wearing Guard clothes, and it was jingling something in its hand. It was no big trick spotting us under the glare of those lampposts, and, sure enough, the Guard did spot us. It opened its mouth in shock and started shouting "BLAH! BLAHBLAH!" Typical human stuff.

"Run!" shouted Skink, but he needn't have bothered, because Chim and I, we were already charging away as fast as our legs could carry us, which was very fast indeed.

TEN

I DON'T know how long we ran—it seemed like forever—and when we stopped, my heart was thudding like this, *baBUM baBUM baBUM baBUM*. My breath sounded all wheezy, like I was some kind of little old monkey. Chim and Skink, they didn't sound much better.

I took a look around. No one had followed us; there were no humans hot on our tails. We were on some kind of road, but much bigger than the one that ran through the Enclosure. There wasn't much else around—a low wall on either side of the road, and beyond them just these big flat spaces. I couldn't see much in them, because there was only one lamppost to light the place up. I wished there were some trees around—it's nice to have a few branches between you and the sky, especially at a time like this.

"Well, what now?" I said.

Chim didn't hesitate. "We've got to go back! The Tribe'll be missing us by now. . . . The Council will be going crazy. Kalibak will be doing his nut! You said we wouldn't be gone long . . . you *said*. We did what we set out to do."

I looked at Skink. My mind was a blur as I tried to make sense of what had happened. I had expected the crocodile to tell us that bits of the Tales were not true—to tidy them up, I suppose. That way, we could have gone back to the Tribe and argued that Skink should not be punished for speaking against the Tales, because even the Tales were not exactly right.

I hadn't expected the crocodile to tell us that we monkeys hadn't been behind the Fence for all that long. Or that there were lots more monkeys who lived outside the Fence. Lots of different kinds of monkeys, too! Or—worst of all—that humans had put us behind the Fence for entertainment! I had grown up believing that humans were our protectors. . . .

Skink seemed to guess what I was thinking. "Look, Kaz," he said, "you can't go looking for the truth and then complain when you find it. Anyway, the crocodile didn't tell us everything—he couldn't wait to eat us. But remember what I said about the chick inside the egg? Well, we're outside the egg now! There's a whole world to explore here. If you want to know where you came from before the Fence, this is where you'll find out." He waved his arm to indicate the huge world around us. "I mean, isn't this what you always wanted? To see the world of humans?"

Before I could answer, Skink gave me a sly look. "Besides," he added, "now that we're here, we might be able to have some fun with them. . . ." Something about what he said unlocked a thought in my brain. My head was full of confusion, but there was something else there as well, something new and shocking: anger—anger at the humans. . . .

"We'll go on," I said at last. "We can't stop now— not until we know everything." Chim let out this great big sigh, but he said nothing.

In the distance, more lampposts were twinkling, and we set off in that direction. Before long, we began to pass these big box-shaped buildings on either side of the road, which Skink said were houses. They looked sort of like the sleeping huts back in the Enclosure, only way bigger and grander. You couldn't see anything in most of them, but then we passed one house where you could see a few humans inside. They were sitting on this *furniture* stuff and their faces were lit up by a bluish white glow from the corner of the room. One of the humans was asleep; the other had its eyes open, only it looked like its brain had switched off or something.

"That's the thing I was telling you about," Skink snorted. "Television. They just sit around in *chairs* and stare at it."

We stood there in the darkness, looking in at those humans slumped in their chairs.

"Now tell me," said Skink, and there was a kind of sneer in his voice. "Does that look like the top of the Tree of Life to you?" I had to agree it didn't.

A noise from behind startled me. It was one I knew well, but that didn't stop me from being scared. A car! It roared by us, and we ducked down so we couldn't be seen. It was going so fast, we needn't have bothered. Skink watched as it sped off, and a slow grin crept across his face.

"Now there's an idea," he said. "We need to get ourselves *motorized.*"

Whatever *that* meant.

The three of us waited behind the bushes. We all knew the plan—Skink had only gone over it three million times for us. We were at the edge of a big wide area, which was called a *parking lot,* which was next to a *supermarket* . . . which was a big kind of *store* . . . which was a place where humans went to get food and stuff. Phew, hope that's clear!

It was getting cold. "How long's it going to be?" I grumbled.

Chim chipped in with a little cry of "I'm hungry." It sounded sad there in the darkness and made me want to hug the little monkey, only of course I didn't, not going in for all that sappy stuff.

"Ssshhh," hissed Skink. "There's one coming right now."

I peered through the bush. He was right—there was a human and it was heading this way. It was carrying something in each hand—*bags,* said Skink. As I watched that human lumbering up, I felt a rush of anger toward it and all its kind. How had I been so stupid to think of them as our protectors—the first and wisest of all the animals? Pah! Now, when I looked at this human, I saw something very different —the clumsy waddle, the stupid clothes, the smug, smooth face.

The human got to its car, shifted both bags to one hand, and pulled out a bunch of bright jingly things—*keys* they were, and Skink had already explained that this was what we needed to get.

"Now?" I whispered.

Skink shook his head—not yet. The human fumbled around for a minute in that clumsy way humans have, then it used the keys to open up a car door.

"Now!" roared Skink, and he charged forward, flailing his arms like a wild thing, which is what he was. I followed, then Chim. The human looked up and saw three screaming monkeys flying through the air. It got this amazed look on its face, and it opened its mouth into this O shape and went, *WAAAAAH!* I would have laughed, only I was busy tugging the bags out of its hand. Chim was standing on the human's shoulders, tugging away at its hair, and Skink was working on the other hand, the important one because it held the keys.

The human was letting out this weird wail now, like *YEEEEEEEEEEE!* and I figured it wouldn't be long before other humans came to see what was going on. But then Skink raised one hand in triumph and shouted, "Got 'em!" I saw the flash of a shiny object in his hand. The keys! I dropped to the ground, and Skink did, too. That's when the human decided enough was enough—it let out this final scream, spun round, and started running back toward the lights of the supermarket. There was just one problem—Chim was still on the human's shoulders! He was too afraid to leap off.

"Jump, you idiot!" shouted Skink.

"Jump, Chimmy, jump!"

A horrible picture popped into my mind—the human charging into the supermarket, which was full of other humans, with Chim still perched on its shoulders! What would they do? Just then Chim came to his senses. He let go of the human's hair and flipped off to the ground. The human ran on, and Chim scuttled back to where we stood by the car. I was worried to see how frightened and confused he looked. I reached out and tousled his topknot, but he didn't offer up much of a smile in return.

"Okay, what now?" I said to Skink.

"Into the car, quick," said Skink. "It won't be long before more humans are back. . . ."

So we piled into the car, and took up our positions, just as Skink had instructed us. There were a couple of short sticks poking out from the floor inside. Skink said they were called *pedals,* and he gave us the proper names—*accelerator* and *brakes,* I think it was. To make things easier for us, he said one was the speed stick and one was the stop stick. I squatted down by the one on the left, ready to work it with my hands. Chim squatted next to me, ready to push down with his fist on the speed pedal whenever Skink gave the word.

Skink stood upright on the chair, which is where humans normally sit down in the car. His job was to turn the big wheel thing, which you used to point the car, *the steering wheel.* First he put the key into some little hole and turned it. The car let out this great big roaring sound, *VROOOOM!* We were ready to go!

Skink fiddled with something around the steering wheel, and the car began to move slowly forward. He cried out for Chim to press down on his pedal. He gave it a good old shove, and the car lurched forward. "Not so hard!" yelled Skink.

Chimmy pressed a bit more gently this time. "That's it! Keep it like that," said Skink, and we were off. It wasn't so tough, this driving business, with me and Chim skulking on the floor by the pedals, and Skink shouting out instructions. Sometimes he would shout out "Faster!" and Chim would press a bit harder. Sometimes he'd shout "Brakes!" and I would push on my pedal. We soon found out it worked best if Chim eased off, too, when I was pushing the brakes.

I couldn't see anything, stuck down there by the pedals. Chim, either. We could just *feel* when the car was going faster or slower. But Skink could see everything on the road ahead, and he gave us this running commentary, so we'd know what was going on, as well.

"Okay, we're out of the parking lot, we're on the street. . . . A touch faster, Chim! Lots of houses and shops on both sides of us. . . . Tiny bit faster! . . . Not many humans out on the streets, though, they must know what's good for them, *heh, heh, heh.* . . . Brake! Not so hard, Kaz. That's it. . . ." He kept it up, on and on like that, telling us what he could see.

Chim had more work to do than me, and I spent a lot of the time just watching Skink. His face was mostly in darkness, but just every so often it got lit up by a light outside and I caught a glimpse of him. The weird thing was, although his voice sounded as cocky as ever, that wasn't how Skink's face appeared. There was something about him that looked . . . well, *lost,* I suppose. But then his face was plunged into darkness again, and we were back to just hearing that voice, full of the same old bluster.

Suddenly Skink called out for us to stop. I hit my pedal. We slammed to a stop and went pitching forward. *Thud!*

"Ow!" cried Chim.

"Smooth brake control!" said Skink.

I rubbed my head, which had a nice big bump starting to grow on it, and asked where we were.

Skink twisted round and grabbed something from the backseat of the car—a piece of human clothing, which he said was what they wore around their necks in cold weather. A *scarp*? No, a *scarf,* he said it was called. Skink opened the car door.

"Time for some fun!" he said, and he let loose a cackle that made the hair stand on end all over my body.

ELEVEN

WE WERE outside a building, but not a house. I guessed it was another store of some kind, only way smaller than that supermarket place. At the front it had this big window, and inside four or five humans were standing in a line. They looked like they were waiting for something.

"What is this place?" I asked Skink.

The little monkey lifted his head and sniffed the air. "Burgers 'n' hot dogs, by the smell of it," he declared, which didn't mean a thing to me. What were burgers, and what did dogs have to do with it? Skink winked at me. "Watch this."

He hopped out of the car, clutching that scarf thing, and scurried over to the store. He stood up on his tippytoes and tied one end of the scarf to the sticky-out thing on the door, which is called a *door handle.* He pulled the scarf as tight as it would go; then he tied the other end to a post that ran down the building. He made a "Come here, quick" sign to us with his hand.

"What are we doing here?" hissed Chim as we scurried over. He gave me this look like he wasn't sure who I was anymore. The thing is, I wasn't sure myself.

Chimmy looked so miserable and scared, I felt bad for him. But another part of me was itching to see what Skink had in mind. "It's okay," I said. "Surely we can have a bit of fun with them just this once? It's only fair." Chim said nothing. We joined Skink outside the store and waited.

It wasn't long before the door shook—one of the humans was trying to get out, but it couldn't because of the scarf. The human tried again, harder this time. The door rattled, but it wouldn't budge. The scarf held fast.

That's when Skink decided to let the humans see him. He popped up in front of the big window and began pulling faces and chattering his teeth at the humans stuck inside. He hammered on the glass with his little monkey fists until it rattled; then he smushed his lips right onto it so that his face looked all weird, and he blew these great big echoing rasp-berries: *PPPPPPAAAARP!*

"*Look* at them!" he shouted. I stood up on my tiptoes and looked in, too. Those humans didn't know whether to be amazed or angry, I guess. A couple of them were tugging at the door now. Their eyes were screwed up with effort and beads of sweat were popping out all over their faces. No luck. The rest of them watched helplessly as Skink hopped around outside.

I didn't know why, but I felt like laughing and dancing myself, like singing at the top of my lungs. No, that's not true—I *did* know why. There was something brilliant about seeing all those humans trapped in there like that—not one of them knowing what to do, not even knowing what was going on. A great big laugh ripped out of me. Chim had joined us at the window now, and even he let out a chuckle. One of the humans inside shook a great big hairless hand at us and pounded on the inside of the window, as if that would scare us away. Yeah, right! It just made us laugh more—in fact, we couldn't stop laughing, because every time we came close to stopping we had another peek at all those helpless humans. We bent double with laughter, and we threw our heads back with laughter, and still it wasn't enough.

I think we might have gone on all night, only we heard this harsh cry from down the street.

"BLAH, BLAH!"

A big human was running toward us. What's more, there was something familiar about this human. With a shock, I realized it was one of the Guards from the zoo. You could tell from the clothes they wore, all the same. Another one appeared, and then several more. I was frozen to the spot, watching them. The first Guard stopped and raised some kind of black stick thing to his shoulder and pointed it at us. There was this loud popping sound and something whizzed by my ear.

That unfroze us pretty fast. Chim and I, we high-tailed it back to the car. Skink followed, but first he cupped his hands over his mouth and shouted at the humans trapped inside the shop: "How do *you* like it, huh?" Then he let out a wild giggle.

Back in the car, we took up the same positions. "Go!" Skink shouted, and Chim pushed down on the pedal. I didn't think we were going to make it. The Guards were bound to get us. Sure enough, a human appeared at the side window. It began pounding on the glass. "Faster!" yelled Skink. Chim shoved harder and the car lunged forward with a horrible squeal. We were off, leaving the Guard standing. Skink was laughing like a crazy monkey. "So long, creeps!" he shouted over his shoulder.

I wasn't quite so happy. "Did you see what they were?" I gasped. "Guards—they must be looking for us. There were *loads* of them. . . ." Huddled beside me down there with one hand on his pedal, Chim let out this little frightened sound, sort of like *eep*.

"Don't worry," said Skink. "We can stay one step ahead of them, no problem."

I wasn't convinced. "What was that thing they pointed at us? That stick thing?"

"A *gun,*" answered Skink. "They use them to kill one another."

Great, I thought, that's just what I needed to hear.

"Like I said, don't worry," he added. "They'll be using special darts for us—ones that send you to sleep so they can take you back. But not me—they're not getting their stinkin' mitts on this monkey ever again!"

There was something about the way he said it— so much anger in his voice—that stopped me asking any more questions. We just drove on in silence, with me keeping a gentle pressure on the pedal now. I was glad that I couldn't see anything outside the car, happy just to let the shadows glide by.

But then: "Hold on, what's this?" said Skink. He had seen something out there. "Go faster, Chim!" Again, Chim pressed harder on the accelerator pedal, and I could feel the car speeding up.

"C'mon, faster!" yelled Skink.

"That's as far down as it can go!" said Chim. I wasn't surprised—it felt like we were going really fast.

"What is it?" I asked.

Skink was hunched forward now, his head and shoulders bobbing up and down with excitement.

"A couple of humans out walking," he gasped. "We're gonna make them sorry they ever left their house! Faster!" He started giggling again—a crazy high-pitched giggle—and when I looked up I saw this wild gleam back in his eyes.

Suddenly I realized what he was going to do. He was aiming the car at those humans! He was trying to kill them! The thought smacked me like a splash of cold water. I knew that Skink was filled with rage against humans—I had shared in those feelings of anger, enjoyed them even—but this was too much for me. I couldn't let this happen.

I hopped up and shouted, "No!" grabbing the steering wheel and jerking it to one side. The car swerved, there was a dreadful screeching noise. Skink began to speak: "What the—" But then the whole car was spinning, and I could hear screaming everywhere, like this *WAAAAAAAH!* only I couldn't tell who it was because all three of us were screaming. And suddenly the whole world was filled with this gigantic sound—*KKKKKRRUUNCH!*—and I slammed forward into the pedals.

I think I blacked out for a instant, and my brain took a moment to get working again. The first thing I noticed was that we weren't moving anymore. The second thing was that I couldn't hear the car's rumble. What I *could* hear was Chim, who was kneeling over me going, "Kaz, Kaz . . . wake up!" and stuff like that.

I sat up and wiggled my fingers and toes. Everything was in working order at least. Skink was yanking the car door open.

"What happened?" I demanded.

"No time," gasped Skink. "We've gotta get out of here *now.*" I could hear why—footsteps in the street, coming our way. Humans! Chim and I, we scrambled out of the door. I looked down the street. Two humans were running toward us. The car was a mess. The whole front end was smashed up against this big old tree. The tree didn't look too damaged, and there was something about that fact that made me happy, like the tree had beaten the car or something.

Skink was already scampering away from the humans. We took off after him. My side was aching with this kind of stabbing pain—I wasn't sure if it was from the crash or whether it was from all this crummy running around we were doing. It didn't matter, though—we were still much faster than those slowpokey humans. I took a glance back and saw they had stopped. They were standing by the car, trying to figure out what had happened and where the driver had gone.

We ran on. We had no idea where we were or where we were going; we just kept on running.

"Gotta . . . gotta stop soon," panted Chim.

But Skink had already stopped and he was climbing up and over some metal fence. I couldn't see what was beyond it, but I knew one thing for sure—it didn't smell too great.

"Where are we?" I asked.

"City dump," said Skink. "We can hide out here for a while. Maybe even find something to eat."

Bing! Those were the magic words for Chim: "something to eat." He began to scramble up the fence, too, and I went after him.

TWELVE

THE FIRST thing we saw on the other side were these two big trucks, and I mean *big*—way bigger than the Guards' trucks. They sat there like they were guarding the place. Past them there were these great big heaps of *something*. I wasn't sure what it was, but it sure stank bad. That's where Skink headed. I held my nose and followed. We made our way along a pathway that ran between the mounds. Soon the lights from the street were far away.

"Poo-ee," commented Chim.

"It's just rubbish," said Skink. "Smells bad, but you can find some good stuff here. It's all the stuff that humans throw away."

He poked at a big black bag, ripping a hole in it. He rummaged around for a while in what spilled out, then said, "See!" In the middle of all the bits of paper and empty boxes and stuff, he had found some food. I peered closer and saw what it was—some grotty old carrots and a few sprouts. They didn't smell the freshest.

That didn't stop Chim. He began to shove food into his mouth. I popped a bit of carrot into my mouth, too. It tasted okay, but I thought to myself, What have we come to, when some stinky old veggies seem like a feast?

"There's bound to be lots more here," Skink was saying. "And better food, too!" He started to head off to explore another black bag, but I grabbed him by the arm. He had some explaining to do first.

"Wait! What was all that about back there?" I demanded. I was feeling pretty angry. "In the car . . . You were trying to hit those humans, weren't you?"

"I was just trying to give them a scare, that's all," said Skink. It was too dark for me to see the expression on his face. Was he telling the truth? How could you know for sure?

"Well, you managed to give someone a scare all right—*us.* What's wrong with you?"

"You don't understand," said Skink quietly.

"What don't I understand?"

"Welcome to the world outside your Fence," he

said, waving his arm as if to indicate the whole world, rather than just this smelly old dump. "Take a look around you, and tell me what you see. It all belongs to humans. What place is there for us? What place is there for any animals? Maybe they're animals that humans like to *eat,* so humans turn them into hot dogs or burgers or something. Or maybe they're animals that humans think are *funny,* so they teach them stupid tricks to do and put them on display in stupid shows. Or maybe they're just neat to look at, so they get stuck in zoos so that humans can come and gawk at them. . . ." He was shouting now, and I could see the blaze of anger in his eyes—stronger than I'd ever seen. "They get shoved in tiny cages, or behind fences, or have their wings clipped so they can't fly away. . . . It's like the fate of every animal depends on how humans view them."

He paused for breath. . . . And that's when we heard it—a scratching sound, like lots of tiny little feet scurrying, and a kind of whispering from all around us. At first it was too soft to make out, but it grew louder and louder, and what it sounded like was: *"Not usss."* But there was nothing to be seen in the darkness.

"Hey!" Chim cried, all scared. "There's something else in here!" The little monkey ran back to where we were sitting. "I don't like this!" he said. "Can we get going now?"

But something told me it was too late for that. The whispering was louder now, still all around us. We were being watched—watched by hundreds of eyes in the darkness. I knew it—don't ask me how, I just knew. I heard the click of sharp teeth, and a hushed laugh. That feeling of panic was back in my belly. I looked to Skink, who got slowly to his feet.

"Who's there?" he said, and for the first time since I'd met him, his voice sounded tired. There was no answer, but the whispering grew stronger. Then at last, something crawled slowly out from the darkness in front of us. It was a rat—a great big one, its fur all tangled and matted, its shoulders hunched over. Even in the dark, I could see hairless patches where deep scars lined its body. Bloodred eyes stared straight at us, and you could tell from those eyes that this rat was smart, but they were hard eyes, and cold, too. Like something was missing in them. We were in big trouble.

"Our place," hissed the rat, only the way it said it sounded like *playsssssssss.* "Thisss is our playss." All around us, the whispers made a spooky echo: *our playsss, our playsss.* It seemed like a thousand shadows were shifting in the dark. I hated to think how many there were of them.

I was on my feet now. "We were just going," I said, politely as I could, and I took a step backward. "We didn't mean to, you know . . . to intrude. We were just—"

"What are you talking about? This isn't your place," cut in Skink, all bitterly. "It's the humans', like everything else."

The rat smiled a killer's smile. "Humans' by day," it said. "At night, our playsss," and suddenly I realized that I could see other eyes in the darkness now, *lots* of eyes, all edging closer and closer.

"Rubbish!" scoffed Skink, and I wondered if he was making some kind of bad joke. "The humans built the dump, didn't they? They bring all the rubbish to keep it going. It's *their* place all right—*you* just live here." I glanced nervously at Skink. What was he doing? This had better be some kind of trick to get us out of this fix, and it had better be a good one. Skink went on: "That's the problem with animals like you. You just live off humans—eating their scraps, and skulking around in their sewers and alleyways. You live in the cracks between human society, and you think you're independent!"

All the while, the whispers around us grew louder and angrier. But we could still see only one rat. That killer smile never faded; those bloodred eyes didn't waver once.

"Anything elssse?" said the rat.

Skink folded his scrawny arms. "I think that just about covers it." And that's when I realized that Skink wasn't going to talk our way out of this one. It was as if he had run out of tricks, and all that was left was the anger, eating away at him.

"Very well." The rat gave a gentle nod of its head, and then: "Now!" it hissed.

There was this terrible shrieking, squealing sound, and dozens of dark shapes flew out of the shadows. Three or four landed on me, and I felt teeth sinking into my fur. I ripped them off and threw them to one side, but more rats were flying toward me. It seemed like they were everywhere, like I was inside a giant mouth full of tiny razor-sharp teeth. Whenever I yanked one off or swatted it away, another two or three jumped forward and took its place. I fell back, and saw that Chim and Skink were covered by our attackers. And even in all that pain and fear, this weird thought floated to the surface of my mind: We survived lions and crocodiles! How could we be done in by a bunch of dirty rats? It didn't seem right.

Suddenly there was a new noise alongside the vicious squealing of the rats—something deeper, a kind of barking. If I say it was sort of *WOOOF!* that doesn't give you the idea of how strong and dangerous it sounded. I raised my head and saw a big animal bound into the middle of all the rats and start tossing them aside with its jaws. Rats began to scatter back into their mountains of rubbish. I grabbed one of the rats on me by the scruff of its neck and hurled it to one side, then another and another.

Rats were scurrying all over the place now, trying to get away from this animal that was growling and howling and having a blast. I ran over to where Chim lay. Two rats were still on him, but it wasn't hard to bash them off. Skink was on his feet, too. More rats disappeared into the darkness.

The big animal trotted over to us. "That was brilliant!" she said with a goofy grin, and her tail wagged like it had an action-packed life of its own. "You three had better hop on board, though. Don't want to be here when Johnny Rat comes back with reinforcements, eh?" The animal lay down so that we could climb onto her back. I got on first, then Skink, and finally Chim.

The animal stood. "Get yourselves a good handful of fur," she said over her shoulder. "It may be a bumpy ride."

And with that, she began to run back toward the entrance of the dump.

THIRTEEN

THE BIG animal had to get out by squeezing through this hole in the fence. Once we were outside, she turned left and began running down the street. I didn't even bother to look where she was going. I wanted to get as far away from that dump as possible, so I just shut my eyes and held on tight.

After a few minutes the animal stopped and crouched down low to let us off.

"Thanks," I said. "For saving us, I mean."

The animal gave this big friendly beamer of a smile, with her big pink tongue all wet and hanging out to one side.

"That's all right," she said. "I like to go chase the rats down at the dump anyway. Tonight, I knew there was something funny going on—I could smell it. No offense." Then she furrowed her brow a little and pushed her big head closer. "Come to think of it, you boys don't look too great, if you don't mind me saying so."

I looked at the other two. It was true—they had cuts all over from where the rats had attacked. I was sure I didn't look any better. Chim looked like he was in shock or something. He had his arms wrapped tight around himself, as if he was freezing. We'd hardly had anything to eat at the dump, and we were cold and tired.

"We're okay," I said. "Just hungry." Then I asked, "Who are you?"

But Skink cut in with "She's a *dog*," and he seemed to be saying the word *dog* like he was spitting out a fish bone, like it was a dirty word or something. All I could think of was everything I'd heard about dogs from the Tales and from what Graybak had told me. I'd formed a picture of the animal in my mind, but somehow the picture didn't come close to this real, living, breathing animal in front of me. She had floppy ears and a long snout, with fur all over it, right up to the nose. She stood much taller than us, and she was a powerful looking animal, good and strong around the shoulders.

"Name's Kayleigh," said the dog, "but my

humans call me 'Peachie.' Don't mind which one you use. Take your pick."

"I like 'Kayleigh' fine," I said, but Skink wouldn't drop it.

"So what do they say to you? 'Go fetch this stick, Peachie,' 'Have a piece of chocolate, Peachie.' 'Good dog . . . *Peachie.*'" His voice was all sneering and angry, and it sure struck me as rude to talk this way to a dog who, after all, had just saved us from about fifty million hungry rats. Still, Kayleigh didn't seem to be bothered, or if she did, she was too classy to let it show.

She twitched her nose a bit and then, looking only at me, said, "Listen. My humans keep the door open so I can get back in the house. We could probably get you boys a bite to eat there. How's that sound to you?"

Was she kidding? It sounded fantastic. We got back on and Kayleigh set off running down the road. Having three monkeys sitting on her back didn't slow her down any. As we made our way, I tried to find out as much as I could about our savior.

"So, you actually live with humans?" I asked. Kayleigh kept on running, but she turned her head a bit so she could answer.

"Sure I do. My family's really neat—they take me to the park twice a day and I get to ride in the car and stick my head out the window, and, okay, they don't like it when I get out and run off down to the dump, but they give me bits of their biscuits and—"

"Whoopdedoo," said a hard-edged voice behind me. Skink. I did my best to ignore him.

"So . . . you *like* being with humans?" I asked. "I mean, you don't ever feel like you should be with other dogs or something?"

"Oh boy, I like it fine with my family," Kayleigh answered. "And, you know, I get to see all my doggy pals in the neighborhood, especially when I slip out without my leash like this." She slowed down a bit. "I suppose sometimes . . ."

"Yeah?"

"Sometimes at night, I dream that I'm running with this giant pack of dogs, and there are no leashes and no rubber toys and no *"Down girl, get off the couch!"*—it's just us, all of us dogs, running free through the woods."

"Sounds great," I said.

"Oh yeah," she agreed. "It's a nice dream. But, you know, real life's not like that. A few of the dogs around here, we really did up and run off to the woods one day. I'll tell you, it wasn't so great. We just got hungry. We tried to catch a rabbit, but it got away, and the only water we drank was this dirty old rainwater, which, you know, tasted yucky. So do you know what I did?"

"What?"

"Ran all the way home, had a great big slap-up dinner of prime dog food in my favorite bowl, then curled up in front of the heater and snoozed right off."

The dog stopped. We were outside one of those house places.

"End of the line, fellas," she said. "This is where I live."

Kayleigh stretched her front paws out and bowed her head down so we could get off again. We were right under another lamppost, which gave us a chance to have a better look at one another. Kayleigh's short fur was a sort of light tan color, and she had a black snout and a big pink tongue. She had this kind, friendly look about her, though I knew there was more to her than that—just ask the rats. She gave us a puzzled kind of look, like she was seeing us for the first time now we were under the lamppost's glare.

"I don't mean to be rude," she said, "but what *are* you boys? I mean, you look sort of like minihumans, you know? Only with tails."

Skink snapped. "We're *nothing* like those hairless freaks! What do you know, anyway?" he shouted. "You're just the humans' pet. You live with them and do what they tell you day in, day out. Bet you roll over and play dead when you want them to toss you a biscuit. . . ."

"Matter of fact, I do. . . . Do you have a problem with that?" A menacing growl appeared in Kayleigh's voice, and I saw that she had a pretty mean set of teeth on her.

"No problem at all," I said, stepping between the two of them. "Don't worry about him"—I nodded at Skink, who was skulking by the garden wall— "we've just had a really bad night, that's all."

Kayleigh nodded slowly, and her easygoing smile returned at last.

"Okay, then," she said. "Well, let's see about getting you that food, huh?" I looked over at the house, where the front door was cracked open just a bit. What lay on the other side of that door?

"But listen," Kayleigh said. "Only one of you can come in, and you've got to be really quiet. Can't let my humans see you, they'd throw a fit." It was clear she felt a lot of loyalty to her human family.

I nodded and stepped forward. Somehow it just seemed natural that I should be the one to go in. The other two didn't seem to mind. They sank down into the shadows under the garden wall so they wouldn't be seen.

"Be careful," said Chim.

"Be quick," said Skink.

Kayleigh began to pad toward the house. I followed, and this thought flashed into my brain: A human house, I'm actually going into a human's house!

FOURTEEN

THE BIG dog pushed the front door open wider with a front paw, and in we went—inside the house. I was trembling all over, partly with fear and partly with excitement. The first thing I noticed was how warm it was in there. The floor felt weird under my feet—all soft and kind of furry, not hard and cold like outside.

"Gotta be quiet," whispered Kayleigh with a wink. She padded along this long, thin room, which she said was the *hall.* I followed her past one door on our left, then another. Kayleigh nodded toward the second door and said, "The family's in there most evenings. It's called the *living room.*" I scratched my head. If that was the area they *lived* in, what did they do in the rest of the house? Humans were a mystery, no doubt about it.

Kayleigh kept going along the hall. I knew I was taking a risk, but I couldn't help myself. I sneaked a peek through the crack in that door. There were five humans in there. They were watching this big box that sat in the corner, making a din, and you could see stuff on it. It had to be that thing Skink had told us about. What was it? Television. Right now it was showing a herd of elephants marching along some sort of great big open space with this spectacular sunset going on in the background. It was weird, because I knew from what Skink had told us that there weren't actual tiny elephants walking around inside the television box. They were just pictures; only they moved just like real life.

I watched a moment longer. Those elephants on the television looked neat, and they didn't look much like the only elephant I'd ever seen, when it had been led past the Enclosure: That elephant, with a Guard leading it along, had been alone and kinda sad-looking.

I looked at the humans in the room. One of them was asleep, its chest rising and falling with these little snoring sounds. Another was saying something—the usual "*Blah, blah, blah*"—but no one answered. A couple of them were little ones, including one that was really little, which was sitting on the floor.

I expected to feel another surge of anger, but somehow it just didn't come. There were so many things about humans I just didn't understand—the way they spoke, their machines, clothes, stuff like that. But what really struck me about these humans now was not how weird they looked, but how familiar. They looked just like a bunch of monkeys all sitting around. One of the little ones was giggling at something, and the way it screwed up its face reminded me exactly of Chim; one of the old humans, which had all this white hair on top of its head, reached over and ruffled the little one's hair, and that reminded me of the way Graybak used to ruffle my fur. This sudden feeling hit me, so strong that it was like a pain in my gut or something—all sad and lonely and homesick.

I felt a nudge from behind. "This way," whispered Kayleigh.

I followed the dog along the hall to another room. She pointed with her snout to some big white box thing that was in the corner.

"That's the refrigerator," she said. "There's food in there, but you'll have to get it. I can't open doors."

I scurried over and pulled the box thing open. A

blast of cold air hit me right in the smacker. I didn't recognize much of the stuff inside, but down at the bottom there was a pile of vegetables and fruit. I grabbed a load, making sure I got enough bananas, which were Chimmy's favorite. Kayleigh showed me where they kept those bag things—you know, like the human at the supermarket had. I grabbed one and stuffed the food in.

"Thanks a lot," I said to the big dog. "For everything."

Kayleigh had been gobbling up this food, which smelled disgusting to me (though, of course, I didn't say that). She looked up at me now and smiled and nodded. Then she said, "Good luck with what you're looking for . . . whatever that is."

"I don't even know," I said glumly. "I don't know anything about the humans' world." I could feel a bunch of hot little tears trying to squeeze themselves out of my eyes, but I told them to get back or else.

Kayleigh swallowed another mouthful of food, then twitched her ears thoughtfully.

"I've got a good friend down the road," she said at last. "She's really smart." Then she added, "She's a German shepherd," as if that explained everything.

"Yeah?"

"Well, one time my family took me to some building in town and left me outside. That's where I met Della, who's the friend I'm telling you about. We got to chatting, and I asked her about this place my family had gone into. Della said it was called the *library*. She says you can find almost everything the humans know in there. If you want to, I suppose."

"But what is it?"

"Not sure, exactly," Kayleigh said. "I've never been inside. But my family always comes out with a load of these things called *books,* so I guess that's what's in there. I tried to eat one once—a book, I mean—but it didn't taste all that good, and my family just got mad at me. But, you know, you might find it more useful." And she told me where this library place was.

I smiled and gave the dog a big hug, gripping her around her thick neck. "Kayleigh, you're brilliant."

"Tell me something I don't know," she said. Then she went right back to her bowl, but I saw her tail was wagging.

Clutching the bag of food, I began to creep back along the long, skinny room. I hadn't gotten far when I heard a noise—one of the humans from inside the living room saying something and then getting up. Footsteps approaching the door. I thought about making a dash for it, but the door to the living room was right in my way. There was no time to head back to the kitchen. I dashed the only way I could go, up these things that I now know are *stairs.*

I heard the human's footsteps begin to clump up the stairs as well. I looked around me. There were three doors leading into different rooms up there. Which one to take? I dashed into the one in the middle. It was a small room, with brightly colored things all over the wall and stuff hanging from the ceiling. And there was a window, which was cracked open just a little. Yes! I started toward it, but then I heard the human footsteps from outside the room getting closer. The door began to open with a creaking sound. No time to reach the window, let alone climb up and out. I leapt into this big wooden thing in the corner that was full of clothes.

Sure enough, the human came right on into the room. It was an adult female and it—sorry, *she*—was carrying the littlest of those little humans in her arms. The child looked all warm and sleepy, with heavy eyes and its mouth yawning all over the place. My hiding place was good and they never noticed me, but I could peek out through the partly closed door and watch them.

The adult human laid the little child down on this big flat thing, which didn't look like much of a comfortable place to sleep—not like up in the branches. Then the adult began to talk and sing in this soft, gentle voice: "*Blahblah-blaaah, blahblah-blaaah . . .*"

Of course, I had no idea what she was saying, but there was something nice and soothing about it. I guessed she was singing the infant off to sleep, and I was struck again by how similar monkeys and humans were. The mothers in the Tribe liked to rock and coo their babies off to sleep. I even had this half memory of my own mother doing the same to me a long time ago—the kind of thing you only remember properly when you're almost asleep, and it gives you a warm feeling in your chest or wherever.

Pretty soon I guessed that the little child had fallen asleep from the way its breathing had slowed way down. At any rate, the adult stood up, took a final look down at the child, and left the room. It was time for me to make like a banana and peel off, as Chim always says. So I crept out from my hiding place and began making my way to the window. I was halfway across the room when this little voice piped up.

"Hello."

It was the human child—the little kid that I thought was snoozing. Well, it wasn't! It was sitting up, with this little smile on its face, looking straight at me.

"Who are you?" asked the little human.

I stopped dead in my tracks. See, there were two weird things about what that little human had said to me. First of all, it wasn't shocked or surprised or anything; it was just asking a friendly question—like it was the most normal thing in the world to see a strange monkey in your room, happens every day. And second—and this was what really amazed me— that it had said *anything* to me at all. What I mean is, that I could understand it! This human girl was speaking in the One True Tongue—the voice of the animals.

"Er . . . my name's Kaz."

"I'm Megan. This is my room." The little human—*she*—smiled a smile as sweet as any baby monkey's. "Do you want to hold my teddy?" She held out this funny-looking thing in her hand—it looked sort of like an animal, only it was all soft and smushy, and I wasn't sure what I was meant to do with it. I found myself scooting over to check the thing out. I gave it a sniff and a shake, but nothing happened. The little human called Megan let out a giggle when I did that—*hee hee hee*.

"What's in your bag?" she asked.

I looked guiltily at the bag in my hand. "Just food."

I was keeping one ear open for the sound of more human footsteps. The last thing I wanted was to get caught in there. "I've . . . er . . . got to go now." I pointed toward the window and edged that way a bit.

A frown of concern appeared on the child's forehead. "You can take Teddy with you if you want," she said.

I still didn't know what the point of this whole teddy business was, but I knew that it meant a lot to this little human. I smiled and said, "Thanks, but no . . . I think it should stay here with you."

And I handed the thing back to her. Just for an instant, our hands brushed together—hers was hardly any bigger than mine, and this thought popped into my head: They're just like us. I moved closer to the window, which was only open a little bit, but enough for me to squeeze through.

"How come I know what you're saying?" asked the little human. "I mean, I sort of understand Mommy and Daddy, but not like this. How come?"

I thought I knew the answer. "A long time ago, I think all humans knew the One True Tongue, but somehow they . . . they forgot it and started to speak other languages—their own languages. But maybe sometimes, when you're *really* little—I mean before you learn the human talk and forget everything else—that's when you can remember the One True Tongue. Just sometimes. Maybe."

Was it true? I didn't know. Back in the Enclosure, I'd heard little humans shouting from inside their cars, and the noise had been as impossible to understand as any other human babble. Maybe the circumstances were just right that night—finding the human at exactly the right age perhaps, or catching her halfway between waking and sleep? I didn't know, but I understood that I'd been given a rare chance that wouldn't come around again in a hurry.

I pulled myself up to the crack in the window with one hand, still holding on to the bag with the other hand. (We monkeys are pretty good at stuff like that.)

"You go back to sleep," I said to the little human. Then I added, "Hope your dreams take you to the Happylands," which is something mothers say to little monkeys at sleepytime.

Then I pulled myself out of the window, out into the cold of the nighttime air. It wasn't just cold, either—it was wet, too. It had started raining, a steady drizzle that made a soft hiss as it hit the ground. I took a last look inside the house. Megan was waving bye-bye with one hand and holding that teddy thing with the other. I waved back just once; then I swung wide away from the window and latched onto this long pipe thing that ran all the way down to the earth. It was pretty easy getting down from that, and then I was back on solid ground. I looked around.

"Over here!" came a whisper in the darkness.

Skink and Chim were still crouched behind the wall. They were wet through. I scurried over and held up the bag, jiggling it so it made this nice rustling sound.

"Food," I said. Chim's eyes went all wide.

We couldn't eat it here, though—it was too bright because of that lamppost. We went on down the road a bit farther and into a clump of bushes in some garden. It was a good spot because we couldn't be seen *and* we got some shelter from the rain.

We began to stuff our faces.

FIFTEEN

THERE WAS plenty of grub. We ate our fill, and then we ate some more. The sound of rain pressed in around us, growing more insistent. We were pretty dry under those bushes, but every so often a big fat raindrop would plop onto the back of your neck. No one spoke. For one thing, we were concentrating on eating. But also it seemed like we were each lost in our own thoughts. Skink hung his head down.

At last he looked up. Our eyes met and we both spoke at the same time, saying the same words: "I've been thinking—"

"Go ahead," he said.

"No, you."

Skink took a deep breath. "While you were inside that house, I was thinking and . . . I wanted to tell you I'm sorry." The bluster was gone from his voice.

Skink sounded bone-tired. He sounded beaten. "When I arrived in your enclosure, I knew it was just part of a big kind of zoo. And I knew I'd go crazy if I stayed there. . . ."

He stopped, waiting for me to figure it all out. It took me a few moments, and then I understood.

"You made Kalibak and the Council angry on purpose, didn't you? You knew what you were doing. And all that stuff about going to see the crocodile and then going back . . ." I said. "You just went along with that, didn't you? Really you wanted to make sure someone helped you get out of the Enclosure. You *knew* we weren't going back . . . didn't you?"

Skink hung his head even lower. "I knew *I* wasn't going back," he said. "But I didn't expect things to turn out this way for you. I wanted you to make your own decision. You've got to believe that, Kaz."

My brain was spinning and I didn't know what to believe, not now. Too much had happened. Skink went on: "But I didn't know everything. I *don't* know everything. I still can't tell you what you really want to know. I can't tell you where you're from. Originally, I mean." He had that lost look on his face again—like the one I'd glimpsed when he was driving the car.

I knew I should have felt angry at him, but I didn't. It was like I'd gone past anger, either at Skink or at humans. In some weird way, I felt stronger than I'd ever felt before, not like the frightened little monkey I used to be. It's hard to explain—I just felt different.

"I'm going to a place called the library," I said at last, and I was surprised to hear the determination in my voice. "Are you with me?"

Both Skink and Chim gave me a nod—we were in this together to the end. I grabbed the bag with what was left of the food and off we went.

We ran through the darkened streets like shadows in the rain. It was late, and no humans were around. Once a car cruised by, but it was easy to duck down and not be spotted. I ached all over, deep in my bones, but I forced myself to run on. It would have been so good just to climb up a nice tree—one that I had known all my life—and just curl up and sleep. It would have been so good to be back home. But I couldn't stop—not now.

The library wasn't far away, just as Kayleigh had said. The building was set back from the road and surrounded by trees. We went closer. A good few of the windows were close to the ground, but they all had these protective grilles on them.

"No problem," I said, and pointed upward. There were unprotected windows higher up that we could get through, and, what's more, one looked to be within swinging distance of the trees. I looked around on the ground until I found what I was after—a nice big stone. I grabbed it and popped it in the bag.

"This way," I said, and began shinnying up the tree's trunk. It felt good to have a hold of bark again—and even better to be in the lower branches of the tree. I looked down to the other two. "Come on," I said. With a jolt, I realized that something had changed: For the first time it was *me,* Kaz, who was telling the others what to do.

While Skink and Chim were climbing the trunk, I scooted along to the outer reaches of the branch. Then I took the stone out of the bag, lifted it up above my head, took careful aim, and threw it straight through the window. There was a smashing sound, followed by a light tinkle as falling glass hit the ground.

I looped the food bag over my shoulder, so that it hung down onto my back. That way I could use both hands. Then I sprinted out along the branch and hopped over, catching the flat ledge underneath the window. I hauled myself up, then poked away the jagged bits of window that were still there.

"Okay." I turned back to the others, who had made it to the same branch. "Now it's your turn."

Once you got through the window, it was pretty easy to get down to the floor. There were these long things hanging down—sort of like really thin branches just hanging straight down. *Ropes,* they were—the humans probably used them to open and close the higher windows. We just climbed down them, hand over hand.

And then we were inside. There were those things called *books* in there—millions of them, all neatly stacked in row upon row of shelves. I ran one finger along a line of them, as if I could get some of their power to rub off by touch alone.

"And each one is about something different?" I asked. It seemed incredible. I pulled one book out. "What's this one?" It had a picture on the front, only this one wasn't the moving kind. It was of some kind of great big truck, but it hadn't any wheels and it was floating on water. It was so big that the humans you could see in the picture looked as tiny as ants.

"That's a *ship,*" said Skink. "They can travel right across the oceans. . . ."

I let out a gasp of amazement. I glanced over at Chim, who was all huddled in a corner of that huge room. He wasn't even bothering to look around.

I went to another shelf. "What about this one?" I asked Skink. This picture showed some human, an adult male, wearing a hat and coat. He was holding something in his hand, which Skink said was another of those gun things he'd mentioned.

"Probably just a story. Humans like to make up silly stories."

As if to emphasize his point, Skink bent the book back. On the inside it was sliced into lots and lots of pieces, all thin as leaves, and each and every one of them was covered with the squiggles of human writing. So that's what books were.

I wandered from shelf to shelf, pulling out more, not knowing what any of them was about or what secrets they held inside. I flicked through a couple, but they too were full of those black squiggles, which meant nothing to me. A depressing thought hit: Even if the answer *was* here in the library, how could we ever learn it?

But Skink hadn't given up. He went from one shelf to the next, until at last he found what he was looking for. He pulled a book out, squatted down on the floor, and began leafing through it.

I went over. "Did you find it?" I asked.

He angled the book so I could see. It had a picture of a monkey on the front, but a different kind of monkey from us—this one had a big red nose, which I would have found pretty funny under different circumstances.

I scooted round and looked over his shoulder as he flicked through the book. This book had lots of pictures on the inside as well, and they were all of lots of different monkeys. Big ones. Little ones. Monkeys with brilliant white stripes down their noses, monkeys with red tufts of fur by their ears, monkeys with dazzling blue eyes. There were tiny furry monkeys, and tough-looking monkeys with big blue butts, monkeys with huge round eyes and monkeys with hairless pink heads. There were monkeys that hardly had any tail to speak of and monkeys whose tails uncurled as long as their bodies. Like the crocodile had said, there were all sorts of monkeys in the world. And that wasn't all. I pointed to one picture of something that was *like* a monkey—sort of—only it had no tail at all and it was *really* big. The creature was poking a twig into an ants' nest while some youngsters of the same kind looked on with thoughtful brown eyes. "Is that . . ."

"It's a chimpanzee," said Skink. I nodded. The crocodile had told us about those, too, hadn't it?

Skink turned a page or two more. More monkeys looking like nothing I'd seen before, and then suddenly I was staring at a bunch of monkeys that were *just* like us. But there was something different here— not about the monkeys themselves, but about where they were: There was no Fence. Instead, it looked like the whole tribe, bigger than ours, roamed free across this wide sweep of scrubby terrain.

Skink looked up at me. So there *were* places where monkeys like us lived free. . . .

"Yeah, but where is it?" I asked.

Skink shrugged and turned the page. He let out this gasp, which was the kind of noise you make when you jump into water that turns out to be much colder than you expected. *AAH!* I looked down at the page in front of him. There was another picture of a monkey like us—this one alone and inside some building—but that wasn't what Skink had seen. He was gazing at the other picture, which showed some kind of human machine. It was a bit like one of those ships, but this one was set against the blackness of the nighttime sky, with only the cold stars for company. It seemed out of place among all these pictures of different monkeys.

Skink did not speak for a long time, and when he did, I hardly recognized the trembly voice that came out. "Before I came to your Tribe, I was in a circus, like I told you. I got to be too much trouble for them, so they sent me off to your zoo." He sighed. "In the circus, we traveled around in these little cages, and every night we had to do these stupid tricks in front of great big crowds of humans. . . . We went from place to place, all over the world, but always doing the same crummy act. The only way I could stand it was to watch humans as much as possible and learn everything I could. But before that, before the circus—"

"Where were you?"

There was this long silence before Skink spoke again. I could hear the wind moaning outside and the rain falling. Inside, I could hear the blood pounding in my head.

"I . . . I don't remember much, except . . . " His voice faltered. "I was a long way from here. I was inside this place, and I was all alone. I knew there were other animals around, other monkeys—I could smell 'em—but I never got to see anyone. I could only talk with those in cages next to mine. You got plenty to eat, though. It was sort of a game. You had a television in front of you and you had to move this stick and all these shapes moved around on the television. When you got it right, you got your grub. There were humans in white coats who came to see me every day. Sometimes they'd have to hold me down so they could poke these pointy needles into me. Those needles—you just never knew what they'd do. Some of 'em were for sucking your blood out, and some of 'em knocked you out cold. Well, one day my cage was opened and a human yanked me out. It was out with the old needle again, and this one sent me straight off to sleep."

In a way it seemed like Skink was remembering all this for the first time—as if he had just unearthed this memory that had been half-buried under all the anger in his mind.

"When I came round, I was in a different place. There was something clamped on my head—I didn't know what—and something else around my body, holding me fast so I could only move my arms and legs. The food system was the same, and food and water arrived in this tube thing that was hanging down near my mouth. It seemed like ages went by, and then there was this giant rumbling sound, so loud that you could feel it in your chest. Then nothing. The days just drifted by, each one exactly like the last. I lost all track of time, what was day and what was night. It was all the same. I don't know how long it was before I was taken out of that place."

"I don't get it," I said.

Skink smiled a grim smile. "I only found out what had happened afterward, when I heard it from the monkeys in the other cages. It was all some kind of experiment, to find out about the effects of something or other up there. . . ."

"Up? You mean . . ."

"Monkey in the next cage said he heard I went right around the world—I don't know how many times. Maybe they used us because they didn't want to risk it themselves; maybe it was just easier for them this way. I was sent up, clean off the Earth, beyond the sky, and up into space. You know what space is? Nothing, that's what, just nothing."

I looked up at one of the windows, heard the rain tapping against it.

"I'm not sure what happened after I got back," he continued. "More tests, more needles, more humans in white coats . . . But I began to plan my escape. I waited and waited. I thought the chance would never come, but then one day it did, when they were moving us to another location. I seized the opportunity. Escaped and went on the run. But I was young; I didn't know as much back then. That's why I got caught. It's a long story, but I ended up in the circus."

The book fell out of his hands and his voice trailed off. He didn't have to say any more. I understood. We're all a part of this Earth, everything that lives and breathes, but Skink had been shot free of that. He had been in the loneliest place I could imagine—he had gone up into the emptiness of the nighttime sky. It was hardly surprising that some of that emptiness had found its way into his heart.

And I realized something else, too: Skink had never known a true home in his life. He had been shunted from one place to another, without ever having a sense of belonging. But me? I had family and I had friends, and a place that was home for me. I felt a terrible longing for what I had left behind, for what Skink had never known. I wanted to be home.

I reached out and placed my hand on his shoulder. I knew it wasn't enough. It would never be enough.

I looked down at the book he had dropped. It had fallen open to a page near the front. Of course,

I had no idea what the writing meant, but it was the picture that left me breathless. It was—

CRASH! The doors into the library burst open. The library was flooded in sudden light, and in charged the Guards. They had found us!

SIXTEEN

FIVE OR six of them burst into the room. It wasn't hard to figure out how they'd tracked us down—the noise of that broken window, probably. They fanned out across the room, making these clumping noises with their great big boots. Some of them were carrying things called *nets,* sort of giant bags made of thin string, which I suppose were for catching us. A couple of the Guards were carrying guns.

I snatched up the book that Skink had been reading, and I stuck it in the food bag. Then I gave Skink this great big shove in the back to get him moving, and I shouted, "Go!" He didn't move at first, but then a dart from one of the guns pinged against the wall near us, and he got going.

We hopped up onto the nearest shelf of books, and then the next and the next, until we were right on the top of the bookcase. I figured we could make our way along the tops right to the rope beneath the open window. But what about Chim? I looked across the room to the corner where he had been sitting. No sign of him—had they caught him? No, suddenly I spotted a small dark shape hurtling across the floor and giving this high-pitched wail. It was Chim.

"Chimmy!" I shouted. "This way!"

But Chim was confused. He started to run one way, changed his mind and went the other. He never saw the two Guards as they jumped out from the bookcase behind him. They each held one side of a net, spreading it good and wide. I shouted out, but it was too late. Before Chim knew it, the net was right over him. He fought like crazy to get out, but it was no good—he just got more and more tangled. At last he stopped struggling and lay still.

"Quick!" I shouted to Skink. We began to charge along the top of the bookcase. When we came to the end of it, we leapt through the air to the next bookcase, then continued running. We zoomed right across the room, hopping from bookcase to bookcase. The humans were barking instructions to one another, and every so often there was the *PFFFFT* of a gun, but still we made our way closer and closer to the window.

We were about to hop over to another bookcase when suddenly a Guard appeared in the gap before us. He narrowed his eyes and raised the gun to his shoulders. But before he could take aim, I reached down and swept up an armful of books from the top shelf. I chucked them straight at him. All those years of throwing clumps of soil at Chim had paid off, and my aim was in. The book hit him head-on, knocking the gun to one side. It felt good, so I picked up a few more books and threw them at the Guard, as well. He bent over and covered his head with his arms and made this sound like *YOW!* I would have gone on throwing books, but I saw more Guards heading our way.

I gave Skink a prod. We jumped right over the Guard to the next bookcase and on toward the window. We reached the wall and Skink went first, scurrying up the rope. I followed as fast as I could, pulling myself up onto the window ledge. Then I turned back and looked down into the library. One of the human Guards was pointing at me angrily and shouting to the others, *BLAHBLAHBLAH!* I stood a moment on the ledge, and suddenly I knew what to do.

I stood upright, tall as I could. Then I let out a great big shout: *WHOOOOOOO-UP!* This whoop was a shout of defiance, and it echoed around the library and said everything that I couldn't hope to put into words. And then I began hopping around and giggling and dancing away. I don't know why, but I knew it was the right thing to do—it felt like the kind of thing Skink would do. When I was sure all the humans had seen me, I jumped out into the rain and the dark.

I had expected him to head for the ground, but Skink was already halfway up to the top of the building. I started to follow. It was easy climbing— lots of good hand- and toeholds, and we were soon up there. I found Skink panting, holding his legs tucked up to his tummy. He looked cold and miserable and wet, but, more than that, he looked small and afraid. It was hard to believe this was the same monkey I had seen standing astride the lion mane, framed against the moon and grinning from ear to ear. But the moon was just a memory—now all we had was darkness and rain, and here we were on the top of a building in the middle of a strange land.

A bunch of pigeons started cooing all indignantly

at the intrusion. I told them to shut up, and I sat myself down next to Skink. He didn't even look up.

"Good idea." I said. "They'll never think of looking for us here."

No answer, then at last: "I don't know what to do. . . ."

I pulled out the book from the bag that was slung around my neck.

"I want you to see something." I opened the book, flipping through as quickly as I could. I paused for a moment at the picture of the chimpanzee. I looked again at that big hand skillfully holding the twig and those eyes that looked so smart and so familiar. It wasn't a monkey, not exactly, and yet . . . I felt like some important idea buzzing around the back of my mind, but I couldn't quite reach it.

The picture I was looking for was not far after the one of the chimpanzee. As I gazed down at it in silence, I knew I hadn't been mistaken when Skink dropped the book in the library. My mind grabbed onto that idea it had been trying to get ahold of, and understanding rushed through me.

"Look." I said. The picture showed all these shapes of various monkeys. We had seen a lot of them in the rest of the book, and there was a chimpanzee there, too. A couple of others were just as big or bigger, and I guessed that they were the gorilla and orangutan. The great apes—that's what the crocodile had called them, wasn't it?—part of our family. And there was one other shape I recognized, too. There, in among the rest of the apes and monkeys, was the figure of human.

I watched Skink's eyes carefully. "Don't you see?" I said. "They're no different from us! We're all related. . . ."

Skink was shaking his head, like he didn't want to believe, but I pressed on. "I didn't tell you what happened back in that house. A human spoke to me—a little girl. She spoke to me in the One True Tongue. I could understand her! I saw what they're like in their homes—they're just like us! They *don't* know everything, and sometimes they do bad things. But there's good in them as well, same as us."

"But it's *their* world," he said. "What place is there in it for us?"

"That's not true!" I shouted. "The world is a huge place, and humans don't run it all, even if they think they do. There have to be places you could get away from them." I pointed at the book at our feet. "We *know* there are. We've seen them, like that tribe in the book."

A tiny spark of interest flickered in his eyes. I went on: "And if any monkey can do it, it's you. You're the mighty Skink! Weren't we supposed to be the lions' supper tonight? It didn't happen, and that's because of you. How about that crocodile? No one else could have done what you did. . . ."

Skink rubbed his chin slowly. "I suppose I *could* do a little traveling," he said. "Move to a warmer climate perhaps—somewhere without all this rain, like in that picture. Who knows?" he said. And then he flashed me one of his big grins. It was good to see it back. "I . . . er . . . don't suppose you'd like to come along with me?" he added.

I shook my head. "I know where I want to be now. With the Tribe—my family and my friends. I mean, what would Chim do without me? I'm going to go back."

Skink nodded, like he had known that would be my answer.

"But," I added, "I'm going to stick around to make sure you get away. Then I'll hand myself in. Deal?"

Skink gave me a friendly swat on the head. "Deal," he said.

I took one last look at that picture in the book. The paper had gone all soggy from the rain, so you could hardly even make it out. I left it up there for the pigeons to coo over, and then we got going.

SEVENTEEN

WE PEERED down over one side of the building. We could see a van in the street below. It had to be the Guards', and that meant that Chim was probably in the back of it. Sure enough, a few moments later the Guards came out of the library and stood in a huddle near the van. They were trying to figure out what to do next.

"The other side," said Skink. We ran across and looked down over there. It wasn't a proper road on this side, just some narrow, dark little passageway between this building and the next one—called an *alley*. It would be risky if we got stuck down there, but it looked like our best bet.

So we climbed down the back of the library building. When we were close enough, we dropped to the ground. I paused for a moment to get my eyes used to the darkness. Then I said, "Which way?" but Skink held a finger to his lips.

The next moment I understood why. We were not alone in the alley; we could hear the sound of breathing, and it was close by. At first I thought it was rats, and my heart jumped. But it wasn't rats. This was the noise of a single animal, and one much bigger than any rat.

That's when we saw the figure lying against the wall. But what? We edged closer, ready at any moment to turn and make a run for it.

The figure stirred and rolled and let out this great big snoring sound, and suddenly I realized it was a human. But what was it doing here? Shouldn't it be sleeping in a bed—you know, inside a house?

We went even closer. The human was bundled up in layers of clothing and lying underneath some kind of shelter. His eyes were shut, and his face was dirty and lined with weariness. His eyelids flickered, and I knew he must be dreaming. What about? I wondered. Probably nothing very different from what we all dream about. Who knows, maybe he was even having a dream about what it meant to have a place called home.

Skink made a signal to me with his hand—he

wanted the food bag, which was still round my neck. I passed it to him, and he reached inside. He pulled out a banana, the second-to-last one in the bag. What's he going to do? I wondered. Some kind of trick?

But it was no trick. Skink just placed the banana carefully on the ground near where the human lay. He saw me staring. "I wasn't all that hungry anyway," he whispered, and that's when I knew Skink was going to be all right.

Then we were off, running down the alley. We made a left turn, then a right. The rain had eased, but the air was still damp and heavy. I was getting exhausted, but I just wanted to make sure Skink got a good head start. Then I could go back to the front of the library, where the Guards were waiting. . . .

At least, that was the plan. But then we turned yet another corner . . . and there were three of the Guards coming our way. They were carrying these bright-light things in their hands and they shone them at us, so that we could hardly see from the glare. One of them shouted to the others. We were about to turn around and scoot back the way we had come, but then we heard the clump of human footsteps from that direction—the other Guards. I ran my hands over the wall to see if we could go up and over. It was no good: The surface was smooth, the wall too high. We were trapped.

As the humans came closer, I felt the fear back, stirring in my guts like an unwelcome visitor from the past. But then I looked at Skink beside me, and I knew I couldn't allow them to take him into captivity again. A new feeling elbowed the fear aside.

No time even to say good-bye. A deafening yell tore from my throat—*YEEEEEEEEEEEEEAAAA-AAAARRRGH!*—and I charged toward the humans. One of them sank to its—*his*—knees and brought the gun to his shoulder. There was another sharp *PFFFT!* and this time the Guard did not miss. Something sharp bit into my shoulder, like an insect bite, but a thousand times worse. My head started spinning, and it seemed like the whole world was wobbling. Just going to sleep sounded like the best thing in the world, but I knew I couldn't give in to that feeling—not yet. I forced myself on. When I was close enough I launched myself through the air at the three humans. I landed on the first, gnashing my teeth and lashing out with feet and fists like crazy. One of the others tried to yank me off, but I sprang high into the air and came back down on *his* head, giving a good tug and ending up with a handful of hair. They were bigger than me, and they were stronger than me—there were three of them, and they were humans, after all—but I battled like a wild monkey. Then the gun sounded again, and a second dart hit me, this time in my chest, and suddenly there wasn't anything . . .

. . . I could do . . .

. . . but . . .

. . . sleep . . .

When I woke up, my head felt like the Big Tree had fallen on it or something. I sat up as carefully as I could. I was in some kind of little cage, but I couldn't tell where.

"Fancy meeting you here, Flea Face," said a voice from across the way.

Chim! Chim was in a cage next to mine. He sounded relieved to see me—almost like his old self, in fact.

"Where are we?" I asked. My head felt pretty groggy.

Chim explained. We were in the back of the Guards' van, which had not moved from outside the library. They must still be after Skink, I thought.

There was only one window in the back of the van, and I had to crane my neck to see anything. I couldn't make out much more than the outline of a few buildings on the other side of the street. The sky was just beginning to lighten. Morning wasn't far off; the darkness would soon be gone.

I watched and waited. We stayed here a long time without moving. I hoped that meant that Skink was far away by now.

"So it's back to the Enclosure . . ." said Chim.

"Back home," I agreed, and I felt no sorrow as I said it.

We heard a *SLAM, SLAM!* then muffled human voices from the front of the van. The van's engine tried to start up, but it wouldn't get going; it just coughed and spluttered.

There was another slam, and I knew one of the Guards was closing a door at the front of the van. A couple of human heads passed by the window at the back of the van. One of them must have bent down, because he disappeared from sight for a moment. He stood back up and he was holding something in his hand . . . something yellow and kind of curvy. Suddenly, I knew what had happened. I started to chuckle.

"What?" asked Chim. "What is it?"

The human was holding a banana in his hand, and he sure looked angry. Skink must have sneaked up and shoved that last banana from the food bag into the van's exhaust pipe.

"It's a good friend saying good-bye." And I smiled.

I poked my head farther up and peered out. Just for an instant, I thought I saw a dark shape moving along the skyline, something small and very, very fast. Perhaps it was just my imagination—you never know—but I like to think that it wasn't.

The van's engine started again, and this time it didn't die.

"Do you think they'll catch him?" asked Chim as we began to move off.

I thought about it—Skink, the tamer of lions, the rider of crocodiles; Skink, the monkey who had seen things hardly any human had seen, then come down to Earth to teach them a lesson or two. I thought of that mischievous grin and the dangerous gleam in his eye. Did I think they could catch the mighty Skink?

"They don't stand a chance," I said.

EIGHTEEN

IT WAS good to be back among the Tribe—good to hear the chatter and small talk as the old-timers yakked away to one another; good to see the little one racing around, driving everyone nuts; good to see the babies riding around, clinging to their moms. Good to be home, although I knew things would never be the same for me here.

Of course, Chim and I were summoned before a meeting of the Council right away. Kalibak wanted to hear everything. He made this big show of acting all furious because we'd broken the Rules, but that's all it was—a big show. You could tell they thought we had been led astray by Skink, that we weren't really to blame. Anyway, the punishment they gave us wasn't so bad—at mealtimes for the next two moon cycles, we had to wait until everyone else had had their pick;

then we got to choose from what was left over. So we got off lightly, and there was only one condition: We weren't to go around telling stories of what we'd seen. Kalibak didn't want us putting ideas into anybody's head. That wasn't a problem for Chim—he wanted to forget it all anyway.

Not long after that Council meeting, it was time for lunch. The food had just been doled out, and monkeys were all over the place feeding. What I really wanted was to go and see Graybak, but there was something I had to do before anything else. Chim offered to help, but I told him that I needed to do this alone. He nodded like he understood, and for once I think he did.

I walked out into the middle of the Enclosure. It wasn't all that hard to spot Blok. He was sitting with a gang of his cronies, shoving food into his face. I went the long way around, so that he didn't see me until the last moment. I stepped right in front of him and the pile of food he was guarding.

At first he tried to come on tough. "So, little Kaz is back?" he sneered, cramming a piece of apple into his mouth.

Blok was as big and strong as ever, but he looked different to me now. I wondered why I had ever been afraid of him. I gave this casual flick of my tail. "You ran away," I said calmly. "You left us with the crocodile. . . ." It wasn't a question, and it wasn't an accusation. I was just stating the facts.

Now Blok couldn't let anyone get away with calling him a coward, especially in front of his buddies. He jumped up; then he puffed out his chest and flattened back his ears and bared his teeth—the works.

I wasn't worried. After what I'd been through, there was even something funny about it. I can't explain it exactly, but I felt like there was a new strength in me, and somehow Blok could see it in my eyes. I walked forward, nice and slowly, taking my time. Blok had to stop himself from taking a step back. I bent down and took a banana from Blok's food pile. According to the Rules, that was just about the worst thing I could do—it was a terrible insult to him. But Blok didn't attack, and I saw why—there was a tiny flicker in his eyes, and I knew that it was fear. I took a delicate nibble out of one end of the banana.

"Not bad," I murmured, and I shoved the rest into my mouth. They all watched me chew, then swallow it in one big gulp.

"You'd better watch your step, Kaz," snarled

Blok, but we both knew that he had to say something like that, just so he could save face in front of his dim friends.

"I will," I answered, and I gave them all a friendly old wink.

Blok shuffled off and his pals went with him. And right then I knew that I'd never have any problems with Blok ever again.

No surprise that Graybak had seen the whole thing. I spotted him watching from over near the huts. For a little old monkey who doesn't get around too well and claims his eyesight's terrible, he doesn't miss much of what goes on. I ran over to him.

"Glad to have you back, boy," he said. Then, so I wouldn't think he was being soppy or anything, he added, "I've been eating terribly while you were gone—thought I'd turn into a darn sprout, I've eaten so many of the things." He ruffled my head, just like I'd seen the old human do at that house.

"So . . . you've been out in the land of the humans, eh?" Graybak said.

I nodded, and then I looked round to check that no one could overhear us. I hadn't forgotten that promise to Kalibak about not telling anyone what I had seen. I intended to keep it, too . . . with one exception. I *had* to tell Graybak, and that's exactly what I did. I told him everything—all the things we had done and all the things we had seen out there beyond the Fence.

The old monkey scratched his grizzled chin and said, "Ah, it takes me back. You know, the things that amazed me the most were the machines. They've got machines to travel around in, and doors that open all by themselves, and gadgets for talking to their friends miles away. It's like they don't do anything for themselves!"

"Yeah," I agreed. And suddenly, I realized what Graybak was saying. A smile danced on the old monkey's lips.

"Hold on! That monkey," I said grinning. "The one who escaped all those years ago . . . It was you, wasn't it?"

Graybak didn't answer—he didn't need to. Instead he said, "Here's something else for you to consider, sonny jim. How do you think Kalibak learned there was a new monkey coming in the first place? Our glorious leader can't understand a word of what the humans are saying."

"You?"

Graybak just smiled again and turned to leave.

"Well, now all that's out of your system, let's hope you can start thinking about the right stuff, for once." He began to amble slowly away, leaving me standing there. He muttered something about his aching bones; then he called over his shoulder, "See you at dinner, sonny boy!"

And that's about it. My tale is all behind me, which is where a monkey's tail should be. I've been back with the Tribe now for three cycles of the moon. Everything's back to normal . . . but everything has changed, if you know what I mean. Chim is still a nutty little monkey, and he's still my best friend, but we don't bother going out and playing on the cars anymore. Leave that to younger monkeys.

I hardly ever look out beyond the Fence anymore, either. Why bother? Seems like there are more important things to think about now. Like what goes on inside the Fence instead of outside. I mean, there has to be a better way to lead the Tribe than to bully everyone into agreeing with you, doesn't there? How about listening to the old-timers, who have got a lot to say if you give 'em half a chance? Or what about working out a new system for mealtimes so it doesn't always come down to biggest and strongest first? Lots of things. I still think of them as my Big

Questions—they're just a different set of Big Questions is all.

The thing is, Kalibak can't lead the Council forever. Soon I'll be fully grown, and I've got this idea to take over as Leader of the Tribe. No, more than that—I *know* I'm going to be Leader. I can feel it in my bones, like some old monkeys can tell when it's going to rain.

For now I'm happy to wait and get myself ready. I spend as much time as I can near the Guards. Most of what they say is the usual old gibberish, but every so often I can make out a phrase or two. Who knows? Maybe the noises humans make aren't so different after all. You never know when knowledge like that will come in handy for when I'm Leader. And, I'll tell you something else—when I *do* become Leader, I'm going start taking all those changes that are only in my brain at the moment and making them real. And, do you know what else? I'm looking forward to it.

Right now, though, as I'm telling you this, I'm sitting up in the Big Tree, just for old times' sake—here in the same old spot where I always used to sit and gaze outward. A few branches above me the sparrows are hopping about their nest and, from the huffy looks they're giving me, I guess they've got eggs in there. I'm no threat, but I suppose Mom and Dad Sparrow aren't to know that, what with being stupid birds and all.

Part of a song floats into my mind, and I find that I'm humming it under my breath. I smile when I recognize it. I take one last look out beyond the Fence, and I wonder where he is, and what he's up to, and what trouble he's causing.

"Take Sim a banana just for me," I sing aloud into the wind.

Then I hop off the branch and scoot down to the ground, because it's dinnertime and I'm starving.

AUTHOR'S NOTE

THE MONKEYS in this story are rhesus monkeys—or rhesus macaques. These are tough little monkeys that are found throughout Southeast Asia and the Indian subcontinent. Partly because of this toughness, and because of their similarity to humans in many ways, rhesus monkeys have been used more often in medical research and experimental studies than any other kind of monkey.

A number of monkeys were used in early experimental space flights also. In 1959 a rhesus monkey called Able was sent up, along with a little squirrel monkey called Miss Baker. When the flight was over, both monkeys were fine, but Miss Baker decided to express her opinion of the matter by biting her trainer.

Monkeys were sent into space much more recently, too, when NASA collaborated with Russian and French space agencies on the Bion Program. One of the program's aims was to test the effects of weightlessness on animals' bones. On Christmas Eve 1996, two rhesus monkeys, as well as many other animals, were launched from Russia and spent two weeks in space. Some scientists considered the Bion experiments a success, but animal rights supporters pointed to the fact that one of the monkeys died before bone samples could be collected. A few months later, NASA withdrew from the program.